# Red Hot ~~Christmas~~

~ The Pride Series ~
Amber & Luke
© 2013 Jill Sanders

### *Follow Jill online at:*
Jill@JillSanders.com
Web: http://JillSanders.com
Twitter: @JillMSanders
Facebook: JillSandersBooks
Sign up for Jill's Newsletter @ JillSanders.com

*Dedication*

To my loyal readers...
Happy Holidays

# Summary

Amber is new to Pride. As the new manager of the Golden Oar, she has big plans for helping make it one of the finest restaurants along the Oregon coast. But when she moves into town, she doesn't count on running into, and almost killing, the most gorgeous man she's ever laid eyes on.

Luke thinks he knows what he wants out of life. That is until the woman he's been waiting for all his life takes him down. Literally. Now he's out to prove he's not just another man-boy, but someone Amber can trust and come to love.

# Table of Contents

# Red Hot Christmas

## Jill Sanders

# Prologue

The wind kicked up as Amber locked the back door of the Casa Del Sol. It wasn't a five-star restaurant, but it had been all hers for the last three years. Well, not hers, but under her command. She'd worked harder than the two owners who were, no doubt, somewhere off the coast of Mexico in the small sailboat they'd named after their restaurant. She'd been left in charge almost two years ago and hadn't really heard from them since, except for an occasional request here and there.

When she'd tried to get a hold of them to request funds to upgrade equipment, it had fallen on deaf ears. To be honest, she'd had enough. The place was starting to fall in, the customers were tired of sitting in ripped booths, and the chefs were tired of working with broken-down equipment. She'd taken this job hoping that she would be able to build the place up to something more. But the owners just seemed to want to squander their profits instead of investing them back into the place to make it something great.

She pulled her coat collar up around her neck as she adjusted her bag and purse. The parking lot was empty except for her white Jeep, which sat at the far end of the lot. She didn't mind locking up by herself; she'd done it many times. She found herself doing it more and more since she'd broken it off with Chris. But she wasn't as enthusiastic about heading home early. The small apartment seemed even smaller. She'd thought about getting a pet to keep her company, but the poor thing would end up being alone all the time.

She walked to her Jeep, keys in hand, as she thought about why she was alone yet again. Maybe it was her? After all, having three boyfriends cheat on you was just a little too coincidental. Right? Tom, the first cheater, had been her high school sweetheart. He was the one that she was supposed to live happily-ever-after with. Instead, she'd walked in on him and her friend Beth shortly after graduation.

Then there was Mike. Sure, she'd only been seeing him for three months. But after seeing him stick his tongue in some girl's mouth across a bar, she'd still been just as upset if they'd been dating longer.

She'd thought better of Chris. Four months ago he'd finally worn her down, and she'd allowed him to move in. Shortly afterwards, she'd realized the mistake. Chris was a man-child. Sure, they were only in their mid-twenties and fresh out of college, but that didn't excuse him from sitting around playing video games twenty-four seven.

She'd leave for work at one in the afternoon and come home at one in the morning, and she'd swear he hadn't moved a muscle. Her couch actually started to smell like body odor, since he didn't shower, but just sat there playing games. It didn't help that a few days after moving in, he'd lost his job at the grocery store.

Still, it had been a huge surprise when she'd come home early one night due to a bout with the flu and had found Chris on her couch with her neighbor Samantha. At the time, she'd looked at it as a blessing. She finally had a reason to kick him out without feeling guilty.

"Woohoo, pretty girl." The deep voice broke her concentration, and she turned around quickly. There were two of them, one on her left and one on her right, making it impossible for her to run away. She gripped her mace key chain close to her and tucked her purse behind her, ready to sprint.

"The restaurant is closed. My husband is going to be here any minute. What do you want?"

"She don't got no husband. I told you, I've been watching her," the smaller one said, holding his hands out so she wouldn't run by him.

"We ain't gonna hurt you—much," the larger one said as he lunged for her. She used her mace on him and kicked the small one in the groin, dropping him as his buddy fought to clear the burning from his eyes.

Then she was in her Jeep and peeling out of the parking lot, vowing never to return.

# Chapter One

The small town finally came into sight after the two-hour drive from Portland. She'd been raised nearby, but the beauty of the area never ceased to amaze her. The trees with their large brown trunks were greener than anything she'd ever seen, as they swayed in the light breeze of the first day of fall.

She'd always lived in the city, but had enjoyed an occasional trip to a state park for picnics or camping with friends. Looking around the small town, she realized this was no picnic. She was here to stay.

She pulled into the small grocery store and looked up at the sign. The words "O'Neil Grocery" hung in new red letters over the white two-story building. The large windows looked into a quaint little store, and she could see people coming and going inside. There were several checkout lanes in the front, and when she pulled into the front parking spot, every eye turned her way.

What was she doing here? She closed her eyes and leaned her forehead on the steering wheel. The memory of those two men, their hands outstretched, walking slowly towards her with laughter in their eyes, made her shiver. She had needed to get out of the city after that incident.

She wasn't going to chance another run-in like that. She knew it wasn't just the city that had thugs, but she'd been thinking of moving for a while. When she'd received the call offering her one of the most sought-after jobs along the Oregon coast, she'd jumped at it. It had only taken her two weeks to get everything in order to move. She was surprised it had been that easy, and it seemed like everything had just fallen in line. Her rent was month-to-month, and she'd easily given her notice for the last day of the month. She'd called around and found the small rental above O'Neil's.

Looking up at the building, she assumed the long stairway to the side led to her new apartment. Putting her best smile on, she got out of her Jeep and walked up to the door. When she walked in, a bell chimed above the door, and she realized every eye was still on her.

She stopped inside the doors and tried not to look nervous. After all, if she was going to be successful here, she needed to win over the locals.

"Hello." She smiled and walked over to a large woman in a bright green dress with yellow daisies on it. "Are you Mrs. O'Neil?"

The woman nodded and wiped her hands on a small white apron. "You must be Amber Kennedy, my new tenant." The last part was said more to the crowd than to Amber herself.

Amber noticed several of the customers' heads turn as they started talking quietly. She smiled and shook the woman's outstretched hand.

"Yes, I've just driven into town. Is this a bad time to show me the apartment?"

"No, not at all." She turned to a frail-looking woman who had been straightening up a few boxes near the front door. "Janice, would you watch the store for me for a few minutes?"

Amber followed the woman outside. "We're so pleased to have you help us out. I know the Jordan's have had their hands full since Lacey and Iian both got married. Lacey's been busy at home with the little one and can't seem to get enough time down at the Golden Oar. Iian, well, he's a superman, and with Allison working from the house he has more time, but he just doesn't like to run the place. He always left the business side to Lacey." She turned and looked over her shoulder as she walked up the stairs slowly. "Lacey's always been the one with the business smarts in that family, at least for the restaurant. Knows how to run the restaurant and the whole family, if you ask me." She turned and walked up the rest of the stairs. "You'll enjoy working for them, sure enough." She took a set of keys from her dress pocket and opened the door.

Amber walked in and smiled. The place was larger than she'd imagined. She walked over to the large front windows and looked out over the main street and the quaint little town she was about to call home. She could just see over the building across the street and saw nothing but the blue of the ocean and the sky. She could make out boats as they came and went in the small port.

She turned and looked at the room. Older hardwood floors creaked under Mrs. O'Neil's weight. To Amber it just added charm to the place. The walls were a nice off-white color with a fresh coat of paint.

"There are two rooms and one full bath. The kitchen has new appliances, just replaced last year after Toby moved out. Toby was the Leif's oldest boy. He was just visiting after his mother's surgery. Nice boy, about your age."

Amber knew Mrs. O'Neil's type. She had matchmaker and meddler written all over her face. Amber smiled and walked past her to get a look at the rooms. One was slightly bigger than the other. The bathroom was very clean and looked nice enough. She could just imagine spending some quiet time alone in the white standard tub, relaxing.

"This will do nicely. The moving truck should be here sometime tomorrow. I've got my deposit and first month's rent." Amber pulled out the envelope from her purse.

"Oh, well." Mrs. O'Neil said, holding her hands together. "We don't have to bother with all that. We mainly just go on the honor system here."

"I'm sorry?" Amber held the envelope.

"Well, I know you've just moved all the way down here. You probably had to pay for the truck and all that. Why don't you just pay what you can, when you can? I don't want you to feel burdened down, financially."

Amber blinked and looked at the woman in a whole new light. Then she smiled. "Mrs. O'Neil, I appreciate your kindness, but this was my deposit from my last place, so it's no burden." She handed her the envelope.

"Oh, well. Okay. But don't get yourself in a pickle. I know young people move around a lot, and it can get expensive. The Jordan's will take good care of you, and if they think that you're trustworthy enough to run their place, then that's good enough for me." She smiled and took the envelope. "Please, call me Patty. Now, did you need some help moving things up?"

"No, I just have a sleeping bag and a few items. Everything else is on the truck, and the moving company will handle all that tomorrow morning." She walked back to the windows. "Is that the Golden Oar?" She nodded towards a large two-story warehouse a few blocks away.

"Sure is." Mrs. O'Neil walked up and stood next to her. "I'm sure you're anxious to go have a look." She looked down at her watch. "Lunch hour is just starting, I'm sure you could get a good look at what you have in store if you swing by now."

Amber turned to the woman and smiled. "You must have read my mind."

Back in her Jeep, Amber watched Mrs. O'Neil walk back into her store and start talking to the same group of women who were still standing there like they had nothing better to do. She knew she needed to embed herself into the tight little community. After all, not just her fate depended on it, but that of the restaurant. She knew from all the research she'd done on the place and the owners that the Jordan's were very tightly knitted into the community. All she needed to do now was to keep her head low and not screw up, and she could be sitting exactly where she wanted to be: managing a highly successful restaurant. It was a job she not only loved, but was very good at.

She was focused on the faces in the market as she backed her Jeep out of the parking spot. She pulled up to enter the street and didn't see the kid until it was too late, and he was flying over the front hood of her Jeep.

Luke took the corner a little faster than he intended and almost rolled the bike. He knew better than to challenge Iian to a race down to the pier, but he just couldn't help himself. Speed was in his nature, as well as Iian's. Iian was smiling at him when he turned the corner onto Main Street, a good two yards ahead of Luke. Luke knew the finish line, the white stripe that marked the pedestrian crossing at the end of Main. They'd been using it since they were ten, when Luke had finally gotten his very own bike. Iian's Skyway bike, dubbed White Lightning, was no match for the Green Machine, Luke's new Haro Freestyle BMX bike.

Since that first summer, the two of them had been inseparable. Now it was a few weeks into fall and Luke was sitting on his gran's porch swing after fixing a few shingles on the roof. Of course Iian was there to help out. After the hard work was done, they sat and talked about the old days. Since Iian was deaf, he leaned on the railing across from Luke so they could use sign-language. Naturally, the bikes came up, since they'd spent half their childhood riding them everywhere.

Luke's bike still sat in his grandparents' garage in like-new condition alongside his cousin's bike, which they kept for when he visited. Blake's bike was a newer model of Luke's Green Machine, but both bikes still shined.

Luke had lived in the large, two-story house just outside of town since his eighth birthday, after both his parents died in a car accident. His grandparents were older, and having already raised their two boys, weren't sure they wanted to start over. But after the tragedy of losing their oldest son, they had welcomed Luke with open arms and hearts.

It had taken a lot of adjustments, not just on their side, but Luke's, as well. He was an only child and was used to having his parents work full time and not give him much attention. But when he moved into the big house, neither of his grandparents worked. Naturally, they hovered over his every move. The bike had been the first freedom he'd tasted since arriving in Pride, Oregon.

It wasn't that they coddled him. They just didn't quite know what to do with him. They finally settled into a pattern and learned the balance of raising another kid while they were in their sixties. His grandfather passed away from a stroke when Luke was twenty-two. It had been a hard blow, to both him and Gran. He'd instantly moved back home from out east where he was attending college so he could be with her. He'd finished his education online and had been working from home ever since.

Recently his gran had mentioned something about winter being around the corner and how the roof above her sewing room had leaked the last time it rained, so Luke had enlisted his best friend, and they'd spent the morning pulling shingles and doing the patch work. It wasn't as if his gran had been in her sewing room for a while, since it was on the second floor. For the last few years, she'd been staying on the main level of the house, due to a hip injury.

While sitting on the deck, Iian had mentioned something about being the fastest in town, and naturally, the challenge was on. At first they had been neck and neck, but then Luke's chain had rattled and no matter how hard he pumped, the bike just wouldn't go the speeds he remembered. Keeping his eye on the chain, he didn't notice the car until he was flying over the handlebars.

Everything went in slow motion as he saw the woman's shocked look as he crashed into the front fender of her Jeep. His first thought was how beautiful her blue eyes were, and how her lips seemed to shine in the daylight. Then he was landing on his back and rolling with the motion of the fall, until finally he was looking up at the clouds. He lay there until her beautiful face appeared above him, her eyes filled with worry. She stood over him and looked down, then her whole attitude changed. Worry turned to confusion, then quickly to anger, and he watched with humor as her hands went to her hips and a small pout formed on her lips.

"What on earth are you doing? Trying to kill yourself?" she scolded.

He lay there in the middle of Main Street and wondered where she'd been all his life.

# Chapter Two

Amber was shocked. Her first thought on seeing the bike and the body was that she'd just killed a teenager. When she rushed to the front of her Jeep and looked down, the first thing she was thankful for was that there wasn't any blood. Then she saw his smile. His dark hair looked messy and long. He wore jean shorts and a white t-shirt that was now ripped along one side. She saw, with great pleasure, an impressive display of muscles that ran along his entire chest and was now exposed. The arms of his shirt strained over biceps that were very impressive.

His copper eyes laughed up at her, and she couldn't control the attitude that came from her mouth.

"What on earth are you doing? Trying to kill yourself?" She stood there waiting for him to stop smiling at her. She looked up and down the street and could just make out another rider at the very end, turning around. Had they been racing? What were full-grown men doing racing BMX bikes through the main streets of town?

"Really!" She held out her hand for him to take it. "You're alright." It was more a statement than a question.

He held up his hand and took hers. His hands were warm, and she felt a spark travel down his skin and up her arm. He purposely put a little extra weight on her arms as he lifted himself up, and she stumbled and almost fell to the ground herself as she helped him up.

"I would think that a full-grown man would know better than to go jetting down Main Street on a bike that's too small for him." She walked over and started looking at the mangled bike. To her it looked like a complete loss. The bike had gotten the brunt of the hit. Her Jeep wasn't even scratched.

He chuckled and turned to look at the mess.

"Oh!" She rushed to his side. "You are bleeding!" She pulled his mangled shirt aside and looked at his back. There were small pebbles embedded in his skin along one side. She tried not to gawk at the beautiful display of toned muscles that ran beneath his exposed skin.

He hadn't said anything yet, and she was starting to worry that he'd bumped his head. So far all he'd done was laugh and smile at her. She took his head in her hands and pulled his face towards her. She remembered hearing somewhere that when someone had a concussion their eyes were unfocused. She pulled his face down to hers and looked into his eyes, looking for any sign of disorientation.

She couldn't see any. His eyes were a copper color that she'd never seen before, and she ended up just looking into them, trying to figure out just how he'd gotten such beautiful eyes. She could see specks of green and gold around the rims. His face was covered with a light stubble that she could feel under her hands, making her want to run her fingers over the slight roughness. Since he was a great deal taller than her five-foot-six frame, he'd been squatting down so she could get a good look at him.

The smile had fallen away from his lips when she'd grabbed his face. Now he just stood there, looking at her like he was trying to figure her out.

There was a cough, and she was shocked to realize someone was clearing their throat as they stood a few feet away. She dropped her hands and

19

backed away from him, tucking her hands behind her back.

"Are you hurt, Luke?" Mrs. O'Neil asked, standing there with three other women. Amber was mortified. They must have run out shortly after he'd done the flip over her car and had witnessed her odd behavior. She could feel her face heating and knew she was red all the way up to the roots of her hair. Taking several deep breaths, she turned away hoping no one would notice.

"Yes, I think I just got cut up a little. I didn't hit my head and don't think I've got a concussion." He looked at her and winked. She felt her face turning redder and looked down at her feet.

"Well, you were very lucky. The last time you and Iian went hauling through town, you both almost got flattened by Mr. Wilkins. You were just lucky Miss Kennedy wasn't moving too fast." The women shook their heads and looked like they all wanted to scold him. "Well, don't just stand there. Go get cleaned up. You're bleeding all over Main Street."

Another woman walked out with a bottle of hydrogen peroxide and some bandages, then handed them to Amber.

"You broke him, you fix him." She smiled and the whole group walked away back into the store, giggling.

Amber turned to him. "What?" She shook her head. "What is wrong with this town?"

He smiled at her. "What do you mean?" He crossed his arms over his chest.

Amber closed her eyes and tried to compose herself. Here she was, minutes after almost killing someone in front of her new apartment, and everyone was more worried about his blood getting all over the street.

"I'm okay, really." He started pulling his bike out from under her Jeep's tire. She looked down at the bottle and bandages in her hands and then looked at his back as blood oozed from the small cuts along his right side. From here she could see tiny pebbles embedded into his skin.

"No, you're not. Listen, why don't you come upstairs so I can clean you up." She nodded to her stairs. "You've got rocks sticking out of your skin. It'll just take a few minutes. Besides, you aren't going anywhere on that. I'll have to drive you home."

He had his bike free and was looking at it. "Man!" He shook his head. "This thing has survived almost fifteen years, a million races, two other fender benders, and being ridden off countless docks into the water." He looked down at the bike with a sad look.

"You seem to be more worried about the bike than the fact that you have rocks sticking out of your back." She walked over and looked down at the ugly green metal. "It's just a bike."

21

"Just a bike?" He looked up at her with shock on his face. "Just a bike!" He picked up the metal and hugged it to his chest. "This is more than just a bike. It's the Green Machine, the fastest bike in town. I won my first race, had my first kiss, and almost made it to second base on this bike." He set the bike down again and looked up at her. "Lady, this is more than just a bike."

She sighed. "Listen, if you don't want me to clean up your back," she said as she tried to hand him the bottle and bandages, "then I will be on my way."

He looked at her hands, then gently leaned the mangled bike against her Jeep, which was still sticking halfway out into the street. "Fine, come on. You can clean me up." He started walking towards the stairs.

"Wait. Shouldn't I move my car?"

He laughed. "Lady, this is downtown Pride, not LA. No one is going to care if you park in the middle of the street." He was halfway up the stairs when the other man came up the road on a silver bike, laughing. She watched as he stopped by her Jeep and looked down at the mangled metal. Then he looked up and moved his hands. She instantly realized he was using sign language, although she didn't know what he was saying.

She looked over, and the man she'd hit—Mrs. O'Neil had called him Luke—was signing back. The pair of them shook their heads like their puppy had just died, and Luke continued up the stairs to Amber's new apartment. She turned and watched the other man ride back up the hill away from town.

She stood there a minute and then the realization hit her: that was probably her new boss, Iian. She knew he was deaf, and how many deaf men could live in one town? Rolling her eyes, she prayed she hadn't damaged her reputation before she even started her new job.

She jogged up the stairs, still holding the bottle and bandages. "Was that Iian Jordan?"

He turned and looked at her. "Do you know Iian?"

She stopped two steps below the landing and looked up at him. "No. Well, I've never seen him before. I had a conference call, well, a text relay call with him. You know, when someone relays for him over the phone. He interviewed me, then we exchanged emails and text messages after he hired me."

"You're working at the Golden Oar?"

She walked by him and used her new key to open the door. "I will be starting Monday. I'm the new manager there."

His eyebrows shot up, and she noticed his eyes scanning her again. Then he walked into her place and stopped. "There's nothing here."

She walked in behind him. "Not yet. I've just arrived. Everything will be here in a truck tomorrow."

She walked into the kitchen and set the bottle down on the countertop. Then she dug in her purse for her manicure set. She had a pair of tweezers and nail clippers that might help pull the pebbles from his skin.

Walking over to the sink, she splashed some peroxide on them to clean them and turned back around. "Well?"

"Well?" He stood there looking at the empty space.

"You'll have to remove your shirt and come over here into the light."

He smiled and slowly pulled his shirt over his head. She held her breath and hoped he didn't hear her heart skip a beat. He was beautiful. She'd never seen someone like him before. He must work out every muscle in his upper body. His shoulders were wide, and she could make out his lat muscles as they narrowed down to his waist. When he walked towards her, he did it slowly, and she couldn't help herself from licking her lips, wanting.

He smiled and stopped in front of her. Then he slowly turned around, and she enjoyed seeing that his lats were well toned. Then she noticed the blood and the pebbles sticking out from his right side. The skin over his muscle and hip was red and jagged with pebbles.

She bent down and got to work pulling the pebbles from his skin. "I'm Amber Kennedy, by the way."

"Luke Crawford."

"Nice to meet you." It took almost fifteen minutes for her to clear his skin of the small pebbles. "I'm sorry about your bike."

"I can fix it."

"That? You can fix that? It's a mess. Why not just buy a new one?"

"I'd never hurt the Green Machine's feelings like that. He's given me plenty of good years. Besides, it's worth a little hard work to make him shine like new again."

"Aren't you and Iian Jordan too big to be riding kid's bikes through town?" she asked after pulling the final pebble from his skin.

He chuckled as he tried to put on his tattered shirt. Then he gave up and bunched it up in his hands and walked to the large windows that overlooked the town. "We normally don't race through the streets anymore, but he double-dog dared me." He turned to her and smiled. "You can't just ignore a double-dog dare."

"How old did you say you were?" She smiled back at him and crossed her arms.

Luke stood across the large empty room from Amber, trying to figure her out. "Why Pride?" Upon her blank look he motioned to the town. "What made you choose here?"

"Oh," she chuckled. "That was easy. Everyone has heard of Iian Jordan and the Golden Oar. Everyone who's anyone in the restaurant business, that is. After leaving my last job, I decided I needed a big change." Luke swore he saw her shiver. "When I started calling around, looking for work, I was ecstatic to receive a call back from Iian, even though communicating with him was a little difficult at first. After we started texting, it was a whole lot easier. I've spent the last week studying basic sign language."

He smiled. She looked like someone who had it all together. Her hair was neatly piled on top of her head, although a strand had come loose when she'd helped him up off the ground. She'd quickly tucked it back under a bobby pin. He itched to get his hands on it to see the length, feel the texture.

"This is a pretty big place to live all by yourself." He started walking towards her, watching her reaction to his obvious question. Her eyes were glued to his chest, and he smiled when he realized she was so focused on his naked body, that she hadn't realized he was trying to see if she was single.

"I have plenty of furniture to fill it. Plus, it will be nice to have a home office." He smiled even more.

"So, there's no one else moving in with you?"

"Hmm?" She finally looked up at his face, and he could see her blue eyes focusing. "Oh, no." He watched her blush again. He'd enjoyed seeing her cheeks turn pink earlier.

"Hmm," he said and stopped right in front of her, just a breath away.

Her chin was turned up, her eyes searching his. He could see the freckles on her nose, then his eyes traveled down to look at her mouth, and he lost his train of thought.

They must have stood there for a few minutes before she blinked and took a large step back. "Well." She cleared her throat. "I hope I didn't injure your ego too much by making you lose."

"Lose?" His mind refused to clear.

"To Iian? The double-dog dare?"

"Oh." He chuckled. "He won't look at it as me losing. After all, I did get to get half naked with the sexy new girl in town."

She blushed again, and he decided it was time to leave. He walked out the door, knowing she was following him. "Besides, his ego could use a little boost right now."

"Why does he need an ego boost?"

27

"Well, when his sister, Lacey, is pregnant, she tends to make things a lot worse for her brothers. Her husband she adores; her brothers she tortures." He smiled. "But you'll find that all out yourself when you meet her."

"I hope she treats her employees like she does her husband."

He laughed and gathered up his bike. "It was nice meeting you, Amber Kennedy. Welcome to Pride. I'll see you around." He started walking, the bike slung over his shoulder like it weighed nothing.

"Wait, the least I can do is drive you home."

"No need. I just live a few blocks away." He turned and started walking again. She watched him disappear around the corner and sighed.

# Chapter Three

Amber decided that visiting the Golden Oar during dinner rush would be just as good as hitting the lunch crowd, since the whole ordeal with Luke had cost her too much precious time. She filled her time until then by dragging her bags and sleeping bag up the stairs and setting everything up. Then she went downstairs and did a little grocery shopping to fill her cupboards.

It ended up taking her a little longer downstairs than she had planned. Patty was not the only chatty one around. She met several other older women who it seemed camped out at the grocery store, since she was sure they were the same bunch that had witnessed her incident with Luke several hours earlier. They all seemed very nice and asked more questions than Iian Jordan had during their brief interview.

The hardest question to answer was if she had any family around. She didn't feel like going into detail about where her father was, and why her mother refused to see her only daughter. So she lied and told them that her parents lived in Portland and were very proud of their only child.

By the time she went back upstairs and arranged everything perfectly in her cupboards, it was only an hour before the main dinner crowd would hit the restaurant.

She decided a slow drive to the building would be just the thing. She enjoyed driving down the side streets of the town and found all the homes completely charming. When she drove up to the restaurant, which sat on the waterfront, she noticed the parking lot was well lit and almost completely full. She was happy to see this on a weeknight.

The building was beautifully remodeled and had new white-washed siding. Large white lanterns lit up the whole front of the restaurant. There was a large hand-carved sign that hung over the front doors. *The Golden Oar* was carved in vibrant gold letters above a large ship with white sails sitting in dark blue waters.

The glass doors had intricate lettering and a sailboat etched in the glass, which shined when she opened the doors. The smells and sounds hit her full blast: warm, rich, family. All sorts of happy sounds could be heard. This was not a white tablecloth dining establishment meant to have quiet voices and pressed napkins. Here, families and couples enjoyed family, friends, and an atmosphere that fit it all.

Smiling, she walked up to the hostess desk. Already she saw things that could use new touches. The uniforms were nice, but with a little updating they would not only have a more modern look, but be more comfortable for the staff. The old computers could easily be replaced with touch screens, which would save time and be more efficient. By the time she was seated, she had a list running in her head of items that could use her touch.

The menus were charming and just needed a little updating. The food list was perfect. She knew Iian ran everything in the kitchen. She'd done a lot of checking up on him and had found as much detail as she could. She knew she would be able to make small hints, but for the most part, would leave everything behind the swinging doors up to him.

She ordered the special of the night, beer-battered fish and chips with a side of clam chowder. She also got an order of the calamari as an appetizer. She knew it was a lot of food, but she wanted to try as much of everything as she could.

She watched how the wait staff moved around, mentally taking notes about which employees worked harder and more efficiently. By the time her food arrived, she knew exactly what her plan would be. When she got a taste of the food, she knew why people drove from Portland to dine at the Golden Oar. The food quality was easily five-star. Now it

31

was up to her to bring everything else in the restaurant up to speed.

When she saw Iian walk out from the double doors, she pasted on a smile. He was wonderful with the patrons. Even though he was deaf, he easily conversed with all the customers and left everyone smiling. He looked like a natural. He spotted Amber and a lopsided smile appeared on his face as he quickly approached her.

"Hello, again," he said smoothly.

"Hello." She shook his outstretched hand.

"We weren't introduced earlier. I'm Iian Jordan."

"Yes, I know. I'm Amber Kennedy, your new manager." She made a point to speak very clearly and face him. She'd done research and knew he could easily read lips, so she wasn't too concerned about how they would communicate.

She watched surprise jump into his eyes, then he laughed and sat down in the chair beside hers. "Oh, boy. I'm going to have fun with this one. It's nice to meet you, Amber. I hope you're finding everything to your liking." He motioned to the empty plates.

"Yes, everything was wonderful. I know I'm a week early, but I figured I'd have some extra time to get settled." She wondered what he meant by, *"I'm going to have fun with this one,"* but didn't want to ask.

"Checking us out, huh?"

"Yes, and so far I like what I see. The food is top notch."

"Well, I'm glad you like it. You just missed my sister, Lacey. She's in the last trimester of her second pregnancy, so I sent her home early. Doctor's orders." He smiled.

"I hope I can get a chance to sit down with her later this week."

"Oh, I'm sure she'll be around. If her husband, Aaron, has anything to do with it, she won't be around too long, though." Amber smiled.

Then Iian leaned in. "I have to thank you for today."

"Today?"

"Yes, if you hadn't hit Luke with your Jeep, he would have easily overtaken me. Bummed about the bike though." Iian frowned a little. "But he's already talking about making the Green Machine better than before." He chuckled.

"Yes, well, I guess I'm not used to two grown men flying at me on BMX bikes." They both laughed.

Luke looked at the digital clock on the wall and wondered what Amber was doing. It was a quarter past midnight, and he was deep in work. He loved this time of night, when everything was still and quiet. His gran was asleep downstairs, and he could focus one hundred percent. He knew he needed to look for his own place, but her health had been failing in the last couple years, so he stayed close. After all that's why he'd come back to Pride. That and his work.

He looked down at the screen and fixed another line of code while thinking about other things. He'd gotten so good at his job, he hardly had to work at it like he had a few years back. Now it just came to him, flowing from his fingertips. He didn't mind the long, odd hours. Being able to set his own schedule made it easier on him. Besides, it left him free to fix his gran's roof, race BMX bikes through town, or flirt with the pretty new girl in town.

He smiled. Yeah, he'd have to make more time to do that again. He was sure she had been into him as well. He'd seen the looks she'd given him, since he had been giving her the same looks back. It had been some time since he'd felt that pull of attraction. Not that he'd been dead since leaving the city, but Pride had limited stock. After all, he'd gone to school here and knew everyone in town and considered them all very good friends. It was hard to find someone you not only found attractive, but were interested in. He'd sure felt both for Amber. He could tell she was the type of woman who had to have everything in order.

It had been pure torture feeling her fingers on his back as she'd meticulously removed every pebble.

He had enjoyed her smell and her feel, and had wanted nothing more than to see what she tasted like.

Shaking his head, he realized he'd been sitting at his computer for several minutes without seeing the screen. At this rate he'd never get his latest job done. He worked through the rest of the night and decided to stop by tomorrow evening and see if the newest member in town needed anything.

The next day it was past noon when he finally woke up. His gran was in the kitchen watching the news on the new flat-screen TV he'd hung on the dining room wall as she baked something that smelled like heaven. He walked up behind her and kissed her and wrapped his arms around her.

"Morning, Gran."

She smiled and smacked his hand out of the bowl she was stirring. "Well, it's about time you got up." She turned and upon seeing what he looked like, started tsk-tsking him, as she was famous for. "One of these nights you are going to have to actually get some sleep. You look terrible."

He hugged her again and this time was successful in dipping his finger in the brownie batter. Sticking his finger in his mouth and licking the sweet goodness, he smiled. "It's not my birthday."

"Oh, you boy!" She cleaned off the drop of mix that he'd spilled on her countertop. "You be a good boy and go clean up. I have an errand for you to run today."

He smiled at her and left the room. If his gran asked him to jump the Grand Canyon in a run-down VW Beetle, he'd do it.

"Oh!" she said as he walked out. "Wear something nice. Not just jeans and a t-shirt."

"Yes, ma'am." He frowned and hung his head as he walked back up to his room. Something nice to his gran meant dress slacks and a button-up shirt. He hated wearing dress slacks and a button-up shirt.

An hour later he walked back into the kitchen where she was sitting at the table. A large covered dish sat in front of her on the table as she read the newspaper. When she looked up at him, she smiled and nodded her head.

"Good, now be a good boy and take this down to that nice young girl that almost flattened you in Main Street yesterday. We need to welcome her properly into town." His gran pushed the container of brownies towards him.

"Gran, are you sure she gets the whole batch?" He looked at her, pleading with his eyes.

"Yes. If you want some, you'll just have to invite yourself in and ask her." His gran went back to her reading, dismissing him.

He stood there and looked at her gray head and realized she was more of a meddler than he had ever believed. How had she known about the incident with Amber yesterday? It must have been Patty. Patty O'Neil ran the local market for one reason and one reason alone. And no matter what she said, it had nothing to do with it being in her family for several generations.

Sitting in his truck outside Amber's apartment, Luke looked at the pan of brownies and swore to himself he'd get some. He peeled back the cover and looked at the iced goodness. His gran made the best brownies in Oregon. When his stomach growled loudly, he decided that it was now or never.

He walked by the large windows to Patty's store and noticed the woman's head turn; her eyes followed him to the side stairs that led up to the apartment. He smiled and waved as he walked by. No doubt she'd be calling his gran to confirm that he had made it there with the whole pan intact.

He stood on the small landing and was about to knock when the door flew open. If he hadn't ducked in time, he would have gotten a large spider in the face.

"Oh!" Amber squealed and almost fell flat on her face. He reached out, and making sure not to drop the tray of brownies, steadied her by grabbing her waist. "My goodness! I almost threw that thing in your face."

He chuckled. "I know, I was there." He looked down at the small dust pan she held in her hand. It was squashed between them. The brownie pan was off to the side, sitting on his hip.

"Do you always throw spiders at guests who bring you gifts?"

"I didn't see you." She looked up into his eyes, not moving.

"Well, that's because you need to look out your door before you toss helpless bugs to their deaths."

"Helpless? That thing was not helpless. Besides, can't they make little parachutes and fly? I think I read that someplace." Her eyebrows squashed together and her bottom lip pouted out in concentration. "Or shoot webs and swing off them like Spiderman?"

He chuckled and shook his head. She smiled up at him. They stood there for a minute like that until his stomach growled, reminding him why he was there.

"My gran made you some brownies to welcome you to town."

"Oh! How wonderful." She didn't move. He smiled even more.

"Can I come in? I haven't eaten anything, and well, I was hoping to mooch some of these off you."

She laughed. "Sure." She pulled out of his arm easily and walked back through the door, setting the dust pan down by a broom and mop. He noticed furniture and boxes were piled around the room in neat stacks.

"The moving guys made it okay?"

"Mmmhmm." Her back was to him as she pulled a few paper plates from her cupboards, which were already neatly and completely stacked. Yup, he'd pegged it; she was a tidy one. Probably had everything organized by color in her closet and drawers. The image, of course, made him think of what kind of silky things would be in those drawers. He tilted his head and looked at her backside, imagining.

She was wearing tight gray legging things. He wasn't sure what women called them, just that they were tight and that he always enjoyed seeing women wear them. Her brown shirt was too long to allow him to spot a panty line, but he imagined she wore silk. Tidy women usually like everything nice and…tidy. She probably had a matching bra and panty set. He liked it when a woman's fun clothes matched. Especially if they were red and lacy.

"Hello?" Her voice broke into his thoughts, and he realized she was standing right in front of him holding out a large brownie on the plate.

"Oh." He cleared his throat and took the plate. "Sorry, I was up late and this is my breakfast." He motioned to the brownies.

She looked shocked. "It's almost two o'clock in the afternoon. And you can't have brownies for breakfast."

39

He took a big bite and smiled, then licked his lips, and said, "I just did."

Her nose crinkled, and she looked like she'd smelled something sour. He almost laughed. "Besides, my gran told me I could if it was okay with you." He took another bite and closed his eyes with the rich goodness.

# Chapter Four

Amber watched Luke with amusement. "How come all grown men act like children around brownies?" She took her plate and fork and took a bite. The brownie was delicious and was still warm and gooey inside.

"You can't eat my gran's brownies with a fork." He walked over to her, picked up the brownie with his fingers, and took another bite. Then he looked at her and waited. Not wanting to offend him, she picked the brownie up and bit into it. He was right, somehow it tasted better.

"So, how did it go yesterday at the restaurant?" He smiled and she felt a little flutter in her stomach that had nothing to do with the chocolate goodness.

"How did you know I stopped by the Golden Oar?" She took another bite, then walked over to

41

grab a few napkins from the napkin holder on her new countertop.

"It just goes to figure. You're a neat and tidy person. I could tell right away. I figured the concern and dedication you have towards your job would pull you down there."

She nodded, "Why do you think I'm a neat and tidy person?"

He laughed. "Lady, look around. The moving company was here less than two hours ago, I'd wager, and already this place is neater than most lived-in homes."

She did look around. To her this was a mess. Boxes lined the walkway, some still packed with items she hadn't had time to put away yet. Her furniture was temporarily placed, since she'd have to wait until all the boxes were gone before making the final decision on where she wanted everything. She hadn't even begun to unpack in her bedroom or office yet.

"I started in here."

He chuckled. "Don't look offended. It was meant to be a compliment. Take me for example. I'm a neat freak with the exterior of a slob. No matter what I do, I can't seem to find what I'm looking for. But everything I have is well cared for, meticulously so."

"Like your bike?"

He thought about it. "Yes, I suppose so. But it took me five minutes to find my keys before I could leave the house."

She laughed, then pointed to her key bowl. "That's why I have one of those. I once looked for my keys for almost two hours, only to find them in the freezer."

He smiled and finished up his brownie. "Well," he said, looking around, "what can I do to help you unpack?"

She stopped, the next bite of her brownie in mid-air, as she looked at him. He began rolling up the sleeves on his dress shirt.

"I don't need any help." She set her brownie down.

"Listen, if you kick me out of here too soon, those women downstairs will call my gran. And you don't want to know the yelling I'll get for not helping a lady move in when I've been asked to bring a tray of brownies over here. We were a package deal, brownies and physical labor."

She looked around for something mundane that he could do. "Um, I suppose you can break down the boxes and put them out in the closet on the back porch area."

"Good." He rubbed his hands together and slid a small pocket knife from his back pocket.

"Did you dress up so you could come down here and help me unpack?"

43

"Yup, gran's idea. She'll use any excuse to get me out of jeans and a t-shirt." He turned and got to work breaking down the empty boxes.

Amber watched his back and wondered what it would take for her to get him out of all of his clothes. She stood there for a minute remembering what he looked like without his shirt on. Then she remembered that he'd said he'd been up all night. Probably playing video games like Chris used to do. Her mind sharpened, and she realized that he was a grown man living with his grandmother. He'd probably been kicked out of his parents' place. He'd also been racing a BMX bike that was too small for him down the middle of Main Street. She mentally crossed him out of her mind. There was no way she was willing to try another man-child relationship, not at this point in her life. Walking into her bedroom, she got to work emptying the boxes and organizing her closet.

The next few days were filled with more unpacking and exploring the small town of Pride. Not that there was much to explore, but they did have a nice library and a couple shops along Main.

She enjoyed walking along the piers, watching the boats come and go. She'd talked to more people in the last two days than she had the entire time she'd lived in downtown Portland. People stopped her as she walked and asked her questions, talking about the town and everything and everyone in it.

It seemed to her that everyone mentioned Luke during their conversations, almost like the whole town was trying to set her up with him. Was he that big of a loser that he needed the whole town to help him get a date? She didn't think so; he'd made a good first impression on her. But after the seventh person brought up his name, she began wondering and decided the best course of action was no action. She was here to stay. It wasn't as if she had to make any decisions. He hadn't even asked her out. So, armed with the new plan of just being friends until he proved his worth, she smiled and was courteous to everyone who spoke to her.

Several people stopped by and delivered food. Most of the well-wishers stayed and chatted about the town and the people in it. She heard all about how the restaurant had been renovated, and about how the Jordan siblings had lost their father and Iian had lost his hearing, something she had read on the internet in an old news article. People couldn't stop talking about Lacey's husband, Aaron. He was the doctor in town since his grandfather's retirement a few years back.

She stopped by the restaurant often and had even taken a notepad once to write down some things she wanted to find out. She still hadn't met Lacey. It seemed every time Amber was there, Lacey had just left at Iian's request.

It wasn't until the night before she was supposed to start working that she finally met Lacey Stevens. Amber had walked into the grocery store to get eggs for her morning omelet when a very small, but very pregnant woman walked in pushing a cart with a little dark-haired girl in the seat. The whole store seemed to hush when the woman entered. The shoppers went around making their purchases without all the chatter Amber had witnessed several times before.

Amber decided to step forward and say something, but Lacey had already spotted her and had headed in her direction.

"Amber?" Amber noticed that the little girl Lacey was pushing squealed happily when they approached.

Amber nodded her head. "You must be Lacey Stevens."

"Yes, and this little one is my daughter, Lillian." The little girl waved her hands and said, "I'm three," over and over again. "Yes, Lilly is three," Lacey said laughing.

"I've been wondering when I'd run into you. It seems every time I stop by the restaurant, you've just left."

"Yes, well, you can thank my brother and husband for that. They keep ganging up on me. I've heard wonderful things about you. I'm sorry I wasn't able to interview you and greet you myself. My brother decided to take the reins on all this since I've got a little one who likes to interrupt phone conversations."

"That's alright. Iian and some of the staff have shown me around. I'm feeling pretty confident about my first day tomorrow."

"Good, if there is anything—"

"I'm two," Lilly broke in holding up five chubby fingers. They both laughed.

It had been almost a week since he'd seen Amber. It wasn't that he was ignoring her or trying to avoid her, but he had a big project going that demanded all his time and attention. The first night he was free, he got dressed up and took his favorite girl out for a fancy restaurant dinner.

"Gran, do you want a booth or a table?" he asked, walking next to his grandmother, holding onto her arm.

"Oh, let's see." She glanced around. "A table would be nice. Maybe one over there." She pointed to the section overlooking the water, right by the fireplace.

The hostess walked them to a cleared table and they sat down as his eyes scanned the dining area. Finally, after they'd ordered, he saw Amber come out of the back doors with a large tray in hand. She helped another waitress hand out the dinner plates for a large group. He noticed her movements were smooth, and her smile was always in place. She

47

looked totally at ease doing the job. Once the table was served, she walked over to the hostess and talked with several people who had just come in. It took her almost five minutes to finally see and acknowledge him.

When she did, she walked over to their table, smile still in place.

"This must be your grandmother. I haven't gotten a chance to thank you personally for the wonderful brownies." She shook his gran's frail hand.

"Oh, well, aren't you a sweetie." He watched his grandmother smile at him across the table. He wanted to roll his eyes at her, but he knew better. She had that sparkle in her eye that told him she was up to her matchmaking ways. His gran was part of the town group that had set up so many other young couples in town. At least they liked to think they'd had a hand in pairing them up. There was no way he was going to fall for her tricks. He knew them all.

"How's work going?" He smiled and decided a quick change of subject was in order.

"Well," she said, looking around, "I can't wait for this training period to be over. I know it's standard to allow me to get familiar with everything, but what I really want to do is get my hands dirty and start making some improvements." She smiled. "But you don't want to hear about my boring job. Oh, look, here's your food now. You two enjoy your meal. It was nice meeting you, Mrs. Crawford."

With that she walked off smoothly as their food arrived. He smiled at her backside as he watched her hips sway.

"The last time someone looked at me like that... Well, let's just say it was a very long time ago. Now, get your eyes off that pretty girl and on your food and eat up." His gran smiled across the table at him. He thought he saw a hint of sadness in her eyes.

Reaching across the table, he squeezed her hand lightly as he smiled at her. "What are you talking about? Men still look at you like that."

She laughed and swatted his hand, then they started enjoying their dinner.

When he arrived home later, there was a slew of messages on his opened chat session. It seemed the new deadline for his current project was in two days. Now, instead of taking his time, he'd have to pull an all-nighter and cram for the next two days to get it all done. He loved his job and working for himself, but at times he wondered why he did it. Then he would sit down and start to create his worlds, and he would remember why he did it. Not only was he good at it, he really enjoyed it.

If you would have asked him in high school what he wanted to be, the last thing he would have said was a graphic designer and programmer. Not only did the job not exist fifteen years ago, but there was

49

no way he would have said he could sit still long enough to create anything.

ADHD had been a huge hindrance in his school work, not to mention the dyslexia that ran in his family. His grandfather and father had struggled with it their whole lives. Sometimes he had to step away from the computer screen and run around the block, just to stay focused.

The weekly basketball games with Iian, Aaron, and a few other guys also helped center his mind. Lately, they had added a few new members since some of the old school buddies had moved away. Since the Coast Guard had set up shop in Pride a few years ago, they'd had their pick of new comers who wanted to take part in a high-impact game of basketball, where you would usually walk away with a bloody nose or a fat lip.

He smiled remembering the last game and how he'd taken Allen, one of Pride's newest residents, a tough coast guard pilot and ex-Navy Seal, to his knees. Yeah, the games were a great way to blow off some steam.

But this week he'd have to work extra hard if he was going to make the standard Wednesday game at the Boys and Girls Club. He had his room all setup for the long haul and got to work. He surfaced a few times when his gran called him downstairs to eat, and he showered to refresh himself once. But for the most part, he spent two straight days working his butt off. When the project was done, he slept for twenty-four hours and woke a few hours before his game with the guys.

Knowing he had a whole month off before his next project was due made him smile. Yeah, this was the reason he worked for himself. That and the money that sat in the bank, untouched for the most part since his return home. When he'd moved back home, he'd started paying his gran's bills, but she'd gotten wind of it, and he hadn't heard the end of it for weeks. He knew she was financially stable, even after his grandfather's passing, but that didn't stop him from trying to help her out. Instead, he did little things around the house that needed to be taken care of. He even took on the bigger jobs like the roof and staining the back deck. She was always there watching over him with a plate of cookies or—god willing—brownies.

He looked down as his stomach growled. "No brownies for you. How about we stop by the Golden Oar for a sandwich before the game?" He rubbed his stomach as he walked out the door and thought about seeing Amber again.

# Chapter Five

Amber was covered in garbage. Well, not covered, but she had bits of trash in her hair and on her clothes. She'd never been more embarrassed in her life as when she'd walked back through the back door of the restaurant, and everyone in the kitchen had started laughing at her. When she saw Iian's face, she knew she had just been accepted into the family at the Golden Oar.

She smiled and took her bow.

"I'm sorry, we couldn't resist." Iian smiled and handed her a clean uniform top. "You can go clean up in my office. There's a sink and towels in there." He chuckled.

She squinted her eyes at him, realizing she would have to pay more attention to him and making a mental note to be leery of any "extra" tasks he asked of her in the future.

Walking past him, she grabbed her bag and went into his office to start changing, mentally checking off the task of taking the trash out on a very windy day, especially on a dock right on the ocean.

It had been a little over a week since she'd first moved to Pride and she'd known that the initiation was coming, just as with any restaurant. She'd enjoyed the job and the people so far and knew that most of them were kind and fun to be around. At least this time she hadn't gotten locked in the freezer for ten minutes like she had at her last job.

She set the extra shirt down and took off her dirty one, which was covered in god knows what. She smelled and wanted a shower very badly, but she still had three hours left in her shift. So she walked over to the large countertop and looked at herself in the large mirror. Yup, she needed a shower. There were bits of trash and food in her hair. Taking a towel down, she decided to dunk her whole head under the sink to try and remove the smell and debris. As she washed her hair, she thought about how her apartment was coming together. She really enjoyed living in the small town. Being above the only grocery store had its perks. She found herself sitting in the living room looking out the large windows, watching people come and go. It helped her in her job, when those same faces came into the restaurant. It almost made it feel like she knew everyone. She would go out of her way at work to ask names and remember them. She'd finally unpacked the last of her boxes the night before and was thankful that the place finally felt like her home.

Amber was bent over the sink and had gotten most of the junk from her hair when she heard the door open and close. Twisting, she saw Luke leaning against the door, his arms crossed, a large smile on his face.

"Got hit with the trash trick, huh?"

She went back to washing her hair with the liquid hand soap. "Do they do that to everyone?"

She heard him laugh and walk closer. "No, just those who are new to town. Most locals know better than to try and do anything during high winds."

She was having a hard time getting her whole head under the running water. She twisted her neck around, trying to let the water run down her left side, moving her body at an odd angle.

"Here," he said as he stood behind her. His hands started to gently rub her scalp. "Let me help you get it all." She felt him picking something out of her hair and closed her eyes. Then his hands were massaging soap into her hair, and she thought she'd died and gone to heaven.

She stood there, her hands braced on the edge of the countertop, dreaming of how it would feel to have his hands run all over her. The clean smell of the soap mixed with his scent almost sent her over the edge. It had been months since she'd been touched by a man and just the thought of it had her squirming. She tried to move her mind in a different direction, but then he moved ever so slightly so that his thigh brushed up against hers.

She was wearing a pair of black leggings, so she could almost feel the heat coming off his legs. She thought about standing between her legs, how it would feel to have him holding her hips as he moved behind her. She almost moaned, but caught herself. His fingers were moving gently over her hair, and she could hear her heart beating erratically as she imagined what she wanted him to do to her.

When he was done scrubbing her scalp clean, he cupped his hands and started to rinse the soap from her hair. She tried to steady her breathing, to slow it down and think of something different, anything but how wonderful it would feel to have him touch her.

Then he turned off the water and handed her a towel. She dried her hair and wrapped the towel around her head. When she stood up he was smiling at her, and then he chuckled.

"What?" She looked at him, thinking that he looked sexy in a pair of old jeans that were torn at one knee. He had on an old MIT sweatshirt that had seen better days. She wondered if he'd visited the campus to get it. "What's so funny?" She took the towel off her head since it was making her feel a little weird. She tossed it on the countertop and started finger combing her hair, trying to get her mind off the fact that she had almost had an orgasm a second earlier.

"You. You're standing there trying to act like you're not as affected as I am." He was still standing close, and when she went to cross her arms over her chest, she realized that she was standing there in her black, nearly see-through bra and her skin tight leggings. She was practically naked. Her face turned red, and she moved to grab the uniform shirt that Iian had given her.

"Oh, no." He blocked her by taking hold of her arm and standing between her and the shirt. "Don't get all shy on me now." He brushed a strand of wet hair away from her face, then he cupped her face and pulled her closer. When their lips met, she swore her eyes crossed, and she could feel goose bumps rise all over her skin. His fingertips lightly ran down her neck as his hot mouth took her breath away. Slowly he backed her up until she was against the marble countertop. He took her hips and pulled her up so she sat, legs spread, on the counter. Then he pulled her close as he stood between her legs, all the while his hands roaming slowly over her exposed skin.

She hadn't known a man could kiss like this. Every thought in her head disappeared. Every question she had about him was gone. Only the feeling of his lips, the taste of him, mattered. She arched her body into his and felt his arousal tight up against his jeans, against her core, as he pulled her closer.

She'd never wanted something so badly as to be able to let him take her here, now. But then there

56

was a loud crash in the kitchen, and she realized where they were. What they were doing. It was worse than having cold water dumped over the both of them. He stood back and blinked a few times. His hands went to his pockets as he looked down at his feet.

"I'm sorry. I didn't mean to..."

She jumped from the countertop and quickly put on the extra shirt, which was a few sizes too big for her. Trying to do everything she could to avoid eye contact, she walked over to the mirror and started to braid her long wet hair.

"Thank you for helping me. Were you here to see Iian?" She tried to regain some of her composure.

He cleared his throat. "Yes and no. I was just having a sandwich before the game."

"Game?" She turned and looked at him.

"Yeah." He smiled as he walked forward and ran the long braid between his fingers. "Iian and I and a bunch of other guys have played basketball down at the B&G club ever since I can remember. That's how I got this." He smiled and held up his arm showing her a scar that ran down the side of his elbow.

"Oh, how terrible." She was shocked that he'd still play after such a bad injury.

"No." He smiled again, "It's wonderful. Like a battle scar. All the other guys are jealous."

She decided then that there was no way she would ever understand men.

Luke took the elbow to the face and twisted a little so he could put his elbow into Aaron Steven's ribs. Both men smiled as they scuffled for the ball. Finally, Luke twisted away, victorious, until Iian materialized right behind him and snagged the ball out of his hands.

Of course, it didn't help that Luke couldn't keep the thought and taste of Amber out of his head. He found himself daydreaming through the game and knew that it was all his fault that his team was now ten points behind Iian's. But at this point he didn't care. He'd purposely chosen not to wager on this game, knowing his mind was somewhere else.

How was he supposed to stay focused when he could still taste her on his lips? He missed a pass from Allen and almost ended up with a ball to the face. Shaking his head, he decided to put all thoughts of the soft, tasty woman he wanted in his bed out of his mind. It worked for all of five minutes.

When the game was done, Allen walked over to him and grabbed him in a neck hold.

"Okay, who is she?" He rubbed his knuckles over Luke's hair, efficiently giving him a noogie that burned his scalp.

"I don't know what you're talking about, bro." Luke tried to get out of the ex-Navy Seal's grip, but the man had arms like vices.

"Yeah, who is she?" Aaron walked over holding the ball and grinning. Aaron was the local doctor in town, but it didn't stop him from playing rough on the court.

Iian walked over with a questioning look on his face. Since no one was signing the conversation, he had no clue what was going on. Finally, Aaron set the ball down and explained, which allowed Iian to get in on the harassment.

"Oh, it has to be Amber Kennedy. You should have seen the two of them sneaking out of my office earlier today. He looked just like you did, Aaron, when I caught you and my sister necking on the couch."

"We never necked," Aaron piped in, signing along.

"Amber, huh?" Allen loosened his grip a little, allowing Luke to renew his efforts to gain his freedom. But Allen tightened his grip again. "Is she hot?"

"She's the new manager at the restaurant. Lacey has been put on house arrest by her overly protective husband." Iian smiled at Aaron.

"What else can she do? Her overly protective brother keeps kicking her out of her own restaurant."

It was an old argument that gained smiles between the two brothers-in-law. At this point, Mark and Steve, their other school friends, walked over to see what was going on.

"Come on, man, let me go." Luke squirmed more, pushing on Allen's back.

"Oh, no. Not until you tell us all the juicy details. They may be happily married," he said, nodding towards Iian and Aaron, "but the rest of us are single and horny. Hey, maybe we stand a chance with Iian's new manager?"

Luke saw his opportunity. He twisted and kicked out, causing Allen to fall backwards. Allen laughed when he landed on the ground.

"So it's that bad, huh?" Allen said, looking up from the ground.

"What?"

"Dude, I can see it. You look just like they did." He pointed to Iian and Aaron who were standing there smiling. "Whipped already." Allen shook his head and got up off the ground, making a show to dust off his shorts.

"I don't know what you're talking about. We've only kissed. It's not like we're dating."

"Oh...," all five of his friends piped in.

If he had known that he was going to get grief over it, he would have skipped the game today. So his mind was on a soft, tasty woman. It wasn't as if he was in love with her. After all, he barely knew her.

Driving home, his mind kept playing over that fact. He knew the next step, if he wanted to get to know Amber better, was to take her out on a date. The problem? There was only one restaurant in town worthy of taking a woman to, and she was the manager there. Not to mention everyone in town would know they were on a date.

So he could take her out to Edgeview, the nearest larger town. There were a handful of nice places to eat there.

When he pulled up to the house, he realized the old place could use a fresh coat of paint. His grandparents had always kept the large Victorian house in its original colors. The tan and green colors were always nice, but now he could see the green trim needed a fresh coat, which probably meant painting the whole damn thing again. The large porch covered a lot of the front windows, and the larger top windows had nice planters sitting just outside on the sills. The front door was the same green, and was half etched glass so you could see the light shining through. It felt and looked like home to him. He couldn't imagine living anywhere else and feeling this peaceful.

Walking into the large entryway, he realized he had a plan. He was going to ask Amber out to

61

dinner. When he walked into the big kitchen off the back of the house, all thoughts of a date vanished as he saw his grandmother lying on the floor. A bowl of carrots lay shattered around her.

# Chapter Six

Luke rushed over to where his grandmother was lying on the kitchen floor and with shaky hands felt her frail neck for a pulse. When he felt the slow beat, he gently shook her, calling her name, until her eyes fluttered open slowly.

"Oh, dear." His gran's voice was weak. "I must have fallen."

"Don't move, Gran." He held her still. "I'm going to call Aaron, and have him come check you out. You stay right here. We don't know if you hurt yourself."

He held her as he reached into his bag and pulled out his cell phone.

Fifty minutes later, Aaron closed his grandmother's bedroom door, and Luke walked him to the living room.

"Well?" Luke asked eagerly.

"Well...I want to run some more tests." His friend took a deep breath. "My initial thoughts are that the cancer is back. But I won't know until after I get this blood work done." He motioned to his black bag. "For now, keep her off her feet, and if she has another spell, call me."

That night Luke sat up in the La-Z-Boy recliner next to his grandmother's bed, watching and listening to her every breath. Thoughts of what he would do if he lost her flashed through his head. When the sun streaked in through her white lacy curtains, the doorbell chimed. His grandmother blinked a few times and sat up.

"Is someone at the door?"

"Yes, I'll go see who it is. You stay right there." He walked down the short hallway to the front door. Standing on the steps of the deck he and his grandfather had built almost ten years ago were more people than he cared to deal with at eight o'clock in the morning.

"Well, don't just stand there, son. Let us in so we can take care of Margaret." Betty, one of his mother's friends, stood on the deck along with at least seven other women, all about the age of his grandmother.

He knew better than to argue with his grandmother, and she was just one woman. To go up against more than half a dozen, well, he would never hear the end of it. So he stood aside and watched the women walk single file into the house. He ran his hands through his hair and wished for a shower and a cup of coffee. Then the smell of something wonderful hit him.

"Is that your coffee cake, Mrs. Lettle?" he asked one of the gray-haired women. She chuckled, then she nodded and held up a large square pan.

"Yes, and you can have some, too...after you clean yourself up. You look like you haven't slept a wink," Patty O'Neil chimed in.

He looked down at himself and saw that he was still wearing his basketball clothes. Then he realized he must stink; he'd planned to shower after he got home from the game, but with all the excitement with his Gran, he'd never gotten around to it.

"Don't eat it all. Promise you'll save me two pieces?" he asked Mrs. Lettle. He knew better than to trust Patty's word. When the older woman nodded again, he smiled and quickly left the room.

Half an hour later, he walked in and saw his gran sitting at the kitchen table, talking to several women. Women were all over the house, cleaning and cooking wonderful-smelling things. How could he complain when he knew this is exactly what they did when someone they loved was sick?

When his grandfather had died and his gran had gotten sick with cancer, the whole town of Pride had shown up at his door. The house hadn't been quiet for weeks. He hadn't minded, and neither had his Gran. She always loved the attention and the company.

He walked up and kissed his gran's cheek. "How are you feeling this morning?"

"Oh, much better, dear. I'm so sorry I've caused such a fuss."

"You never cause a fuss." Mrs. Lettle handed him a plate, and he sat down and ate a double helping of the best coffee cake he's ever eaten, washing it down with two cups of coffee.

"Gran, I'm going to go down and see Aaron. I'll be back soon." He didn't want to worry his grandmother about the tests, but he was anxious to know what Aaron had found out.

"Well, okay, dear. Don't forget your coat. It's going to get colder."

"Yes, ma'am." He kissed her cheek again and left, knowing that his grandmother wouldn't be left alone until she was back to full health.

He walked out the front door, then immediately turned back around and grabbed his jacket from the hall closet. He'd lived here long enough to know when the weather was going to change, and he knew by evening they'd have some snow. Fall was fun on the Oregon coast; you never knew what kind of weather you'd end up with. Those select few who could read it could usually tell, and he was one of those few. By the time he pulled into the parking lot at the doctor's office, there was a light mist on his windshield.

When he walked into the office, he noticed that Betty was back behind her desk in the reception area. The whole room was decorated in Halloween decorations. Ghosts and witches hung from the ceiling, and black and orange streamers circled the room. There were several kids with parents sitting around the room, some with sniffles, some playing quietly with the toys in the corner. He'd grown up coming to this office when Aaron's grandfather had been the town's doctor. Dr. Stevens Sr. had been a great doctor, but Aaron was even better.

When he walked in, Betty smiled at him and motioned for him to sit. Then she got on the phone and called Aaron in the back, telling him that Luke was there. He sat next to a woman, Keri, whom he'd grown up with. She was holding a little girl who was asleep. The girl couldn't have been older than three, and she looked pink in the face.

"Is she running a fever?" he asked.

"Yes, it started late last night. This is the first real sleep she's gotten."

Luke could see Keri was tired, no doubt from staying up with the baby all night. He knew the feeling, but instead of a child, he'd been up worrying about a full-grown woman.

This got him thinking about having children. There was no doubt in his mind that he would stay up with a sick child. His gran was important to him, so he could only imagine what a small, helpless baby would be like. Dark curly hair, big soft blue eyes, little freckles on her tiny nose, covered with porcelain skin. He shook his head realizing the image he'd created was a mini version of Amber.

"Luke?" Aaron walked into the room. "Come on back."

"Why don't you take Keri first? I think her little one is in more need."

"Oh, no. I'm not moving until Riley wakes up. She needs the sleep. You go ahead." Keri kept holding the baby gently and smiled weakly at him.

Once he was back in Aaron's office, he sat down and rubbed his eyes. He felt like he'd been hit with a truck.

"Stress due to worrying about someone you love is a killer. You can't help your grandmother if you can barely stand on your feet. Why didn't you get some sleep last night?" Aaron sat behind his desk and looked down at a chart.

"I grabbed a few hours," he said, looking down at his hands. He knew his friend was right, but he also knew he'd stay up again tonight.

"Well, the blood work that's come back so far all looks good. Your grandmother's counts are right on the mark. I'm still waiting for a few tests to come back, but I think we can rule out that the cancer is back. I'd like her to get a complete physical at the Edgeview hospital once she feels up to it."

"Sure. Can you set that up or do I have to call?" Luke felt like a huge weight had been lifted off his chest.

"No, no. I'll take care of it. How about Friday?" Aaron looked at his computer screen, and Luke sat there while he clicked away. "Friday around one?"

"Sure. I'll make sure we're there." Luke went to stand.

"Luke, if I see you tomorrow and it looks like you haven't gotten at least six hours of sleep, I'm going to have to tell your grandmother I'm worried about your health. Neither of us wants her to worry about you, so get some sleep."

He nodded his head and smiled a little at his friend.

Amber was excited. Tonight was her first official night as manager. It had been two weeks since she'd moved into the small town, and she was more than ready to fly solo. Well, okay, she wasn't exactly flying solo, since there were fifteen other employees

69

on shift that night. Why was she nervous? It wasn't as if she had never managed a restaurant by herself. She'd pretty much acted as owner at the last place, since the actual owners had never been around.

But this felt different somehow. She wanted everything to go smoothly. She'd really come to like the small town and its people over the last several weeks. She found it humorous that she could almost set her watch to the comings and goings of some of them. She knew the patterns of the mothers as they herded their children to school.

She found that she spent more time looking out the large windows in her apartment than she did watching her new flat-screen television. Every time she looked she saw two old men sitting across the way on a long bench just outside the barber shop. They were usually smoking pipes and laughing. They always waved when she stood at the window. At first she was embarrassed that they had seen her, but then they went back to talking like she wasn't there, so she'd made it her habit.

She'd left for her shift a few minutes early and was thankful she had. It was still a week until Halloween, but the snow was coming down quickly. She trusted her Jeep to get her there and back with no issues. She'd just gotten new tires over the summer and knew that everything was in top shape. It took her some extra time making it down the hill towards the restaurant, but only because there was a late-model sedan in front of her that was driving ten miles per hour under the speed limit.

Amber walked through the front doors of The Golden Oar at exactly two o'clock. Taking a deep breath, she made her way to the back room and stored her bag and coat in her personal locker. She chatted with a few employees and waved as Iian headed out the door for the day.

As far as bosses went, he was turning out to be the best she'd ever experienced. He was laid back and still kept all his employees in control. She didn't know how he did it...yet. All bosses had secrets, and she was bound to find his out sooner or later.

By the third hour into her shift, she was ready for her break. When she stepped out back to walk along the dock, something she'd become accustomed to doing during her breaks, the snow was coming down faster and in thick bunches.

Thomas, one of the floor managers, was leaning against the railing, smoking. When he heard her approach, he turned and tossed his cigarette over the railing.

"Hey, out for some fresh air?" he asked leaning against the railing.

He was a fairly good looking man. His blond hair was slicked back, and she could see snowflakes landing on his head and quickly melting.

"Yeah, you never realize how hot it is in there until you step outside." She pulled her jacket closer and tucked her glove-less hands in her pockets. Looking out over the choppy ocean, she took a deep breath and closed her eyes at the wonderful freshness. "In Portland you don't get this."

"What?" he asked. She could hear laughter in his voice, and when she opened her eyes, she realized he was staring at her.

"The freshness of it all." She smiled at him. "Don't get me wrong, it's not like Portland is rolling in smog. It's just that I didn't get to feel the wholesomeness of it all until I came here. Does that make sense?" She laughed at herself.

He chuckled and nodded. "I felt the same way when I came here almost eight years ago." He turned and looked out over the water. "There isn't a day that goes by that I'm not thankful that I came here."

"Where did you come from?" It sounded funny and she realized it the second she said it. Her already flushed face turned even redder.

He chuckled and looked over at her. "Originally, New York. But we bounced around a lot. My father is still pretty high up in the military command. The last I checked, he was stationed in Fort Worth. I had always wanted to find that place, that one special town I could call my own." He smiled. "It was easy to spot when I drove through Pride. I walked into the restaurant that same day and Iian hired me. It helped that my dad had sent me to a special school that taught sign language."

"Oh, you know sign language? I've been trying to teach myself a few phrases. I purchased a book and everything."

"Not working well?"

"No." She pulled her hands out of her jacket and crossed her arms. "I can't believe how hard it is to mimic simple drawings."

"If you want, I can tutor you." He almost laughed at the face she made. "No, I'm not hitting on you. I'm actually in a relationship right now and don't want to do anything to upset him."

Her chin almost dropped; she was lucky she'd caught it in time. She usually had a pretty good gaydar, but this one had jumped out of nowhere. He chuckled again.

"I know, I know. I don't come off as the type." He smiled again.

"Well, personally, I have no problems with it at all, just so you know." She walked over and leaned closer to him. "Now I feel ridiculous for almost having a crush on you." She smiled.

He winked. "Almost?" He laughed as she punched him lightly on the shoulder.

By the end of her shift, her feet hurt, her hair smelled like burnt food, and she felt like she had a layer of grease all over her body. Her mind was focused on one thing and one thing only: getting home and taking a hot bath.

When she started her Jeep, the cold air blowing from her heater hit her full blast. She'd forgotten to turn it off, and she knew that it would take almost two minutes to get warmed up.

When she drove into the parking lot outside her apartment, the snow was almost blinding. She made a run for the door and stopped dead when she noticed Luke's truck in front of her steps. Looking around, she saw that the store lights were all out, since they had closed a few hours earlier. She approached the truck and saw Luke in the driver's seat. His head was leaned against the foggy window, and he looked like he fast asleep.

# Chapter Seven

Luke jumped when Amber knocked on his car window. She almost laughed, but then she got a look at his eyes and saw the weariness in his face. He ran his hands through his hair and opened his door and slowly got out. When he stood next to her, she realized he looked even more tired than she'd thought.

"What's wrong? You look like you could use a good night's sleep."

"Yeah." He rubbed his hands over his neck and looked up at the snow. "Any chance I could come in for a few minutes? It's kinda chilly out here."

"Really?" She gauged him and after a second's hesitation, realized he wasn't trying to use this as an opportunity to hit on her. He looked too tired and beat down for that.

"Sure, I'll make us some hot chocolate." He followed her quietly up the outside stairs. When they entered her apartment, she rushed over to turn up the thermostat. "This place takes less time to heat than my Jeep." She tossed her keys down in the bowl by the door and hung her jacket up on the coat rack. She turned to look at him and saw that he stood just inside the door. He hadn't removed his coat and looked like he had no intention of doing so. "Want me to take your coat?" she hinted.

"Huh? Oh, sure." He removed his jacket and continued to stand in the same spot. "You finished unpacking. The place looks good."

She laughed. "How can you tell? I haven't turned on a light yet." Hanging his jacket up next to hers, she walked over and flipped on the kitchen lights. The room was flooded with warm light.

"Yeah, looks nice," he said from his spot at the door.

"Are you going to come all the way in or stand by the door all night?" She turned and walked into the small kitchen to start heating the water. "Make yourself at home," she called out as she ran the water into the kettle. She listened, but couldn't hear anything from the next room.

When she walked into the living room a few minutes later while she waited for the water to boil, she saw him standing by her windows, looking out at the snow and the town.

"It's a great town." She stood beside him.

"Yeah. I didn't always think so." His hands were in his jean pockets, and he was wearing his MIT sweatshirt.

"Oh yeah?" She turned and gave him her full attention. "Why?" she asked when he didn't say anything further.

He turned and looked at her, then ran his hands over his face and walked over to the couch and sat down. "When I was eight I was in a bad car accident that killed both of my parents." She gasped and walked over to sit next to him. "It took me a while to learn how to walk again. I'd broken both my legs and my collar bone. But the doctors got me back on my feet and shipped me off to some grandparents I'd never met. I was angry that first year. Angry that I'd lived while my parents had died. I guess I took it pretty hard and since my grandparents were the only people around, I ended up taking it out on them. But after a year of very hard labor helping my grandfather rebuild half the house, the anger finally settled down inside me."

She sat there and listened to his story, wondering what he was getting at, not knowing if she should just come right out and ask him what was wrong. But then the kettle whistled, and she went and made them hot chocolate. When she came back in, he hadn't moved a muscle.

After taking a sip, he set it down on her coaster and continued with his story.

"Actually, it was thanks to Iian and some of my other buddies that I finally started liking this place." He chuckled. "I was really angry at the time that the school didn't have a soccer team. After school one day I spotted a few guys playing basketball, and got even madder. I remember walking over there thinking basketball was a wussy sport, and I'm sure I mouthed off a lot to the boys, until finally, they challenged me." He laughed. "Naturally, I lost. I ended up walking home with a fat lip and a loose jaw thanks to how rough the other boys played." He smiled over at her, and for the first time that night, she saw a sparkle in his eyes. "They still play that rough. Anyway, when I'd gotten home, my gran was there with a big batch of her brownies and it finally felt like home."

She reached over and took his hand. "She seems like a wonderful woman. Luke, is something wrong with your grandmother?"

He looked down at their joined hands and nodded. "They didn't think it was the cancer coming back. All the blood work looked good, at first. But then they did a scan today." He closed his eyes, and she could tell it was bad.

"I'm so sorry." She held his hand and wished she could take a little of his pain away.

"They give her two months. That's it. That's all the time I have left with the most wonderful woman I've ever known."

She didn't realize a tear had escaped her eye until he reached up and wiped it away with his thumb.

"I'm sorry. After dropping her off back at home, I just meant to go for a drive. Some of her friends were at the house and they were going to stay with her. Most likely some of them will live there for the next few months until..." He shook his head. "I drove up to the national park, a place I used to go that first year when I was still mad. I thought that the anger would come back, like it did when my parents died, but instead I just felt.... Anyway, instead of driving home, I ended up here."

"When was the last time you had a full night's sleep?"

He shook his head. "Aaron's been hounding me about it as well. I know I have to get my sleep. I plan on trying to get a full night of it after I leave here."

He picked up his cup and drank the rest of the lukewarm hot chocolate in one gulp.

"I'm sorry to come over and dump on you like this. I guess I just needed a new ear. Most of my buddies have wives that would kill me if I showed up at their door at..." He looked at his watch and whistled. "Wow, I guess it's later than I thought. What are you doing coming home this late?"

"I closed tonight. It's not that bad. When I lived in Portland, I usually got home when the sun was coming up."

He stood quickly. "Listen, I'm sure you want to get some rest yourself. Thank you for the hot chocolate and for listening to me ramble."

She stood and followed him to the door. When he opened it and started to walk out without his jacket, she pulled on his arm. "Luke?" He stopped and looked over his shoulder at her. The snow was falling in the background, the street light haloed around his head, and for a second, she lost her train of thought. He was beautiful, and knowing that his heart was breaking for an old woman made him even more so.

She took two steps and walked right into his arms, then stood on her toes and kissed his soft mouth.

At that moment she didn't care that he was a man-child, or most likely going to be another big mistake in her ever growing list of mistakes. The only thing on her mind was the feel of his lips and the sexy masculine smell of him. His hands went to her hips, holding her steady. Then she pulled away and stepped back. Blinking a few times, she remembered her train of thought.

"You don't want to leave without your coat." Walking over, she took it off the hook and handed it to him.

He smiled down at it. "If that's the way you remind people, I'll make sure to leave stuff here all the time."

She smiled. "Go home." She pushed him playfully out the door. "Get some rest. Tell your grandmother I'll be praying for her." His smile faded a little. "If you need anything, let me know."

He put on his jacket and nodded, then disappeared into the dark as the snow silently fell.

The next few days were tough on Luke. His grandmother insisted that they continue with all their holiday arrangements, so he spent all day Saturday arranging and hanging Halloween decorations. Halloween was almost two weeks away and every house on the block already looked ready to spook the neighborhood's kids. The snow had come and gone in two days, leaving everything wet and muddy. He didn't mind, since his truck was built for mudding, another pastime he and Iian enjoyed together. This year, he doubted he'd take any time to head to the hills or the beach to enjoy the fun.

He stayed close to his gran's house, even though he'd been right and there were currently three women staying in the guest rooms. The Henderson sisters—Annie, Amber, and Andrea—looked exactly the same and were too hard for him to tell

81

apart. The only one he could sometimes make out was Annie, since she was the shortest and thinnest of the three. He had no clue how to tell the other two apart. He did everything he could to avoid getting in their way, but he was determined to stick out the next few months with his gran. He wanted to be there for her; he needed to be there for her.

He'd text Iian and tried to back out of the weekly game, only to have Aaron show up on his door step an hour later. The doctor had the stern face down pat.

"What's this all about?" Aaron stood under the deck as the rain pelted down. Luke could barely hear him, so he invited him inside, trying to usher him into the front room so his gran wouldn't hear.

"I'm going to miss the games for the next few months. I think it's best if I stay close to home."

"Luke, you can't be here all the time. You need to get out, be with your friends."

"What I need is to be here for the one woman who gave up everything to take care of me."

"We both know that there is a schedule going around for the town women to sit with your grandmother. It's not like she's alone."

"She needs me right now. I can't just walk away from her."

"You need your own space, some time to blow off some steam."

"What I need is to be left alone."

He didn't mean to raise his voice, but he must have been louder than he'd thought. His grandmother walked into the room, her hands on her hips.

"What are you two arguing about?"

Both men turned to the frail woman, standing in the door. "Nothing." Their heads hung and their eyes were on their shoes.

"Luke?" She stood there quietly until he looked up and into her eyes.

"Yes, ma'am?"

"You'd better run along, or you'll be late for your game. Your gym bag is just inside the laundry room." She turned to Aaron, efficiently dismissing Luke. "Aaron, how's that wife of yours. When is she due again?"

Luke could hear them chatting as he went to retrieve his bag and basketball shoes. How had he been so lucky as to have a grandmother like that?

Later, as Luke was wiping the sweat out of his eyes, he realized that Aaron had been right. He had needed to blow off some steam. He could feel the anxiety leave his body with every rapid heartbeat. If he played a little rougher than normal, the guys didn't complain about it. By the end of the game, he was covered in sweat and he felt more centered than before.

He decided to shower in the lockers instead of heading home.

Living in a house with four older women, no matter how large the place was, made him appreciate the younger of the species even more. These women were very meticulous about their daily routines. He'd always known his grandmother was a stickler, but seeing how the three sisters lived made him think that all women were the same.

He wondered if Amber had a daily routine. What kind of good smelling stuff did she put all over that sexy little body each day to make her smell so good?

After the game he stopped by the restaurant to check in on her. He knew her schedule by heart thanks to someone in the house posting a copy on his refrigerator door. He figured it was most likely his gran, since he already knew she had it in for them.

When he entered the restaurant, the last thing he'd expected to see was Amber dressed in a large, hooped fifties skirt with a pink poodle on it. Her long hair was put up tight in two pony tails that swung around when she talked and walked, and she had on the sexiest shade of red lipstick he'd ever seen. His steps faltered as he walked in and zeroed in on her.

She noticed him and smiled, then executed a cute bouncing walk and came towards him. "It's always fun to dress up the week of Halloween. What are you going to be this year?"

He hadn't thought about it. To be honest, his whole mind had been consumed with his gran's health.

"I can be anything you want." He smiled and pulled his leather coat up like the Fonz used to. He wished he had a comb to grease his hair back. She laughed and held onto his arm, walking him to a large booth near the back wall.

"I could always use another strong greaser." She laughed when he made a funny face. "Well, it was worth a shot." She sat down next to him and opened a menu.

He looked at her, and she looked back. "What? I got off thirty minutes ago. What do you say to a dinner partner? I'm starving!" She leaned closer to him and cupped her hand near her mouth. "I have it on good authority that the lobster bisque is something to die for tonight."

He smiled, he couldn't help it. She looked like she was truly enjoying herself. Scooting closer to her, he put his arm around her shoulders and smiled when she settled next to him. He wished for a quiet, dark dining room instead of a loud one full of families and children, but, it would have to do...for now.

Amber's heart skipped a beat when Luke pulled her closer. Even though they sat in a crowded room, she felt like they were the only ones there. She'd heard how his grandmother was doing from almost every person that came through the door. It seemed that everyone in Pride joined in spreading the word, especially when it was someone they all admired and cared for.

She tried to make the mood light and fun. After all, what else could you do when you were wearing a hooped skirt and ponytails?

She had to admit that by the time both their plates were cleared, she was wishing to be able to spend more time with Luke. He was easy to talk to and funny when the worry left his eyes. When she looked around the room and realized that it was practically empty, she knew she couldn't stall anymore. She'd seen him looking at the clock on the wall, probably worried about getting home to his grandmother.

He held her umbrella over her as he walked her to her Jeep. Then she leaned up and kissed him quickly on the lips, before he had a chance to make a move. "Thanks for our first date, Luke." She smiled and swung her skirt, holding her hands in front of her, and added. "Golly, I hope I didn't get you in too much trouble keeping you out so late."

He smiled. "Next time, baby." He pulled her closer, still holding the umbrella. "Maybe we can take a drive to watch the submarine races out at Lookout Point." He leaned down and slowly kissed her, and she felt herself start to shiver as he ran his free hand over her arm and back. She leaned closer into him and felt his warmth spread into her until her skin was on fire and she was aching for more.

On her short drive home, she kept asking herself why she always did this to herself. She knew what she was getting into. She'd convinced herself not to get involved with him and had even laid out a very sensible plan for how she would accomplish the task. So why wasn't she following her plan?

When she pulled into her parking spot, Patty motioned to her through the store window. She wanted to get out of the uncomfortable outfit, but found herself heading into the store instead of upstairs to shower and change into her yoga pants.

"There you are, dear. I was just telling Ruth here"— Patty motioned to an older woman who nodded and smiled at Amber— "that your parents live in Portland. She thinks she might know them."

Amber felt the blood leave her face as she looked towards the older woman. Was there any chance that she knew her parents? God! She hoped not!

"Regina and Ronald Kennedy?"

Amber took a deep breath and relaxed a little and shook her head. "No, my parents' names are Donna and Frank Kennedy. I think I had a cousin named

87

Ronald." She smiled apologetically and hoped that would be the end of the conversation.

"Oh, well, I know a Donna Kennedy, but she lives in Eugene instead of Portland. It couldn't be her then." Ruth patted her silver hair.

Amber's ears started ringing and she felt a panic attack slamming into her. She had to get out of the store, and soon.

"I'm sorry, Patty, I need to get out of this dress. It was nice meeting you, Ruth." She turned and made it up into her apartment in record time. Her breath was coming in quick gasps, and her head felt light as she slowly sat down, her back against her front door. She folded her legs up and rested her head against her knees.

She'd been running from her family for too long to have them brought up in some small town. How was it possible that someone in this small town knew her mother? No doubt the news would be spread all over town by the morning that her mother was crazy and her father was a terrorist.

# Chapter Eight

W hen she walked into the restaurant just after noon the next day she made a point to watch and see what the reaction was. So far, no one stared at her or whispered in hushed tones while looking in her direction. Maybe that was too high school-ish. She walked into the back room and noticed everyone was moving around, busy as usual. Nobody seemed to care or notice her.

Could she have lucked out? Maybe Ruth didn't know her mother? Maybe it was a different Donna Kennedy?

By the end of the shift, she knew that no one in town knew her story. There were enough locals coming and going each day that she would have had some clue if they knew her secret. But she'd worked herself up so much that morning that she had a migraine by the time she pulled into her parking spot that night.

Jill Sanders

She was happy it was close to one in the morning so the store's windows were all dark. It was one less thing she would have to worry about. But when she entered her place and saw the blinking light on her message machine, she knew her monthly call had come. No matter what she did, her mother always found her phone number.

"Hello, Amber. It's your mother. I wanted to let you know the progress we've made for your father. So far, Mr. Malone thinks we have a chance this time. All we need is your cooperation. If you change your mind about helping out, give Mr. Malone a call. You have his number." The machine beeped at the end of the message.

Amber walked into her bathroom and dropped her hoop skirt and shirt. She pulled the pony tails out of her hair as she turned on the hot water. When it was nice and steamy in the room, she stepped under the spray and cried until she couldn't cry anymore.

Walking out of the bathroom, she wrapped herself in a large towel and fell face first on her bed and didn't move.

*The darkness consumed her mind, and she shivered in the cold. When she looked out the window of the van, she saw a man lying on the ground, staring up at the night sky with empty eyes. She knew the monster was inside the large silver building, but she didn't know when he'd be back. Remembering what had happened just a few minutes ago, she shivered again.*

*"You stay down now, Amber. I mean it. Don't poke your head up for nothing. Daddy's just going to go meet a friend, then I'll come back and take you out for some ice cream, like I promised."* Her father turned his head and waved at someone out of her sight. She was nine years old and sitting on the floor of her father's van. It was a week before her birthday. She remembered because Gabby Luft told her that she wouldn't go to her birthday party if she were the last girl on Earth. Amber had cried all day, and even now her eyes were puffy and red. It was one of the reasons she'd pestered her daddy into taking her on this short trip. He'd finally agreed and promised her that if she was good, he'd take her out to Stripes, her favorite ice cream place.

She'd stayed tucked down on the floorboard of her father's van until she'd heard the yelling. Then she'd quietly stood up and looked out the side window. What she saw changed the way she would look at her father for the rest of her life.

There was a young man in a guard uniform down on his knees as her father stood over him, yelling. The man's blond hair was curly. She remembered that detail because she'd always wanted curly blond hair. His hands were raised up like he was praying, but before she could blink, her father pulled a gun out of his coat and shot the man right in the face. Amber's whole world shattered in that split second. She was frozen in place; even her eyes refused to blink. She watched as her father walked past the man's lifeless body and into the large building. He

91

*was holding the black case he always had hiding in his closet.*

*She thought about running away, about just opening the door and running. But then she looked at the dark heap that used to be a man and realized she was afraid. Too afraid of the monster that was out there.*

*It must have been only a few minutes later when he came back out, but to her it had seemed like years. She could see the monster walking out of the door, moving closer to her. She quickly ducked down and tucked her body into a ball, closing her eyes tight, listening to every sound. She could hear her heart beat loudly as the van door opened, then closed, the van swaying with the extra weight. The monster was inside with her, and he had her father's voice.*

*"See, darling, I told you I'd be back quickly. Oh, here now." Her father reached under her chin and pulled her face up towards his. "What are all the tears about? Are you still upset about what that girl said to you today?" Amber looked up, trying to meet eyes she no longer knew, but her eyes refused to focus on his face. Instead all she saw was a monster she was now very afraid of. So she nodded her head and tucked back into a ball.*

*"Well, don't give that girl a second thought. Let's go get you some ice cream to make everything better." He chuckled as he drove away from the large building.*

In sleep, she mimicked the actions of her nine-year-old self until finally she woke, more tired than before. Rubbing her forehead, she swung her feet over the bed and pulled on a pair of yoga pants and a large sweatshirt. Walking into the next room, she stood at the windows and watched the quiet town. But instead of seeing the dark buildings or the street lights, she saw her father's face.

Halloween came and went quickly for Luke. He coasted through handing out candy with his gran that night dressed as a pirate, a costume he'd used a few years back.

He felt like there was a fog over his eyes. The fact that he hadn't had a good night's sleep since getting the bad news was finally catching up with him. When he sat down with the four women later that night to watch Dracula in black-and-white, he found himself nodding off.

The next few days he watched his grandmother's health deteriorate slowly. At first she had a hard time standing up, so someone had brought her a wheelchair to help her get around the house. He moved all the furniture around so she could easily get everywhere she wanted. Then one morning he noticed that her eyes were not tracking him as he talked to her. He purposely moved quietly across the room, and she continued to speak to him like he hadn't moved.

"Gran?" he said when he made it back to the first spot, "are you having trouble with your eyes?"

"Oh, well, don't worry about that. I'll be fine. I'm just a little tired. I think I'll go lie back down." She moved to push the chair back down the hallway. He was there to do it for her.

"We can go see Dr. Stevens, if you need?"

"Oh, no. I don't want to bother anyone. I'm sure I'll feel better tomorrow."

The next morning, she was still having problems, so he arranged for Aaron to casually stop by before the game that week.

"Mrs. Crawford, Luke says you're having problems with your eyes. Would you mind if I checked on them? I promise no needles this time." Aaron smiled.

"Oh, well, I suppose so. How's that baby coming along? I just can't wait to see it. You're having a boy this time, right?"

"Yes, ma'am. He won't be showing up until after Thanksgiving some time. I know Lacey and Lilly are really excited to see him." Aaron continued to chatter as he looked at Luke's grandmother. Luke didn't like the frown on his friend's face. When they walked outside, Aaron broke the news that she most likely wouldn't gain her eyesight back.

He tried to bow out of going to the game, but his friend insisted that at least he sit on the sidelines and watch. So he sat there for about half an hour, then quietly walked out the doors. He found himself walking around town since the weather was nice enough. He avoided the grocery store and instead headed down towards the docks.

When he reached them, he leaned on the railing, looking out over the water. He had a small sailboat docked there. He hadn't taken it out in months and probably wouldn't for a long time. He just couldn't imagine going out on the water and enjoying himself while his gran suffered.

"Hey." He heard a voice from behind him, and when he looked, he saw Amber walking towards him, holding a small to-go box.

"Hey, yourself." He leaned back on the railing. "Taking a break?"

"Yeah." She stopped right in front of him. "It's my lunch break. Care to join me?"

"Um, sure." He straightened.

"There's plenty here." She held up the container. "Let's go over there." She pointed to a bench and he followed her and sat down. "You're not playing today?"

"No. I decided to take a walk instead."

"Well, you couldn't have picked a better day for it." She took a deep breath and closed her eyes. "I always love the occasional sunny day this time of year."

He looked around and realized she was right. "How's work going?"

"Oh, it's wonderful." She smiled over at him. "I'm still waiting for something to change. I keep thinking there can't be a job this perfect; there has to be something wrong with it."

"Do you always look for the negative in things?" He chuckled as she opened the container of food and saw a huge hamburger. He knew that the restaurant made some of the best, and this one was enormous. She was right, there was plenty of it to go around. It sat on a large pile of spicy fries and there were two large pickles sitting off to the side.

"Mark, the chef on duty, thinks I'm too thin." She smiled. "He keeps giving me too much to eat. Do you know, the other day, he actually made me a whole chocolate pie to take home? I still have several slices tucked away in the fridge."

"Mmm." He looked down at the container, "No chocolate in there?"

She laughed. "No, just one of the largest burgers I've ever seen. I don't always look for the negative, no. I guess you could say I'm just cautious."

"I can see that." He took the half of the burger she offered him and immediately took a bite. He always loved the burgers there, but this one was better than any he'd had in a long time.

"I know. It's crazy, huh?" She handed him a napkin from her pocket and laughed at him.

"What?" He took another bite.

"How good it is. I mean, I've had burgers before, but this..." She held up her half and took a big bite. He watched her eyes close and listened to her moan as she chewed. Then she slowly licked her lips and all thought of food left his brain. He stared at her mouth and was mesmerized. Her cheeks were pink due to the slightly chilly wind coming off the Pacific. Her hair was tied back in a loose braid and tiny wisps of hair framed her lovely face. When she opened her eyes again, he noticed how blue they were today. Almost as clear as the sky itself.

"What?" She took her napkin and frantically wiped her face. "Did I get ketchup on my face?"

He smiled and leaned over to place a soft kiss on her mouth. "No, you look happy and beautiful."

She looked at him, a slight smile on her lips. "Thank you. You look tired."

His smile fell away. "Yeah." He picked up his burger and took another bite. "My gran is stuck in a wheelchair now and on top of it all, she can't see anymore."

"Oh, Luke! I'm so sorry." She reached out and took his free hand. "Is there anything I can do?"

He shook his head and looked down at the rest of his burger half. He was no longer hungry.

97

"Well..." He could tell she was struggling to come up with something else to say.

He jumped in, trying to lighten the mood. "So, do you have family around here?" He instantly regretted it when she sighed and looked off into the distance.

"Yeah. My mom is in Eugene. My dad...isn't."

"Oh?" He watched her nibble on some fries, and could tell she was deep in thought. "You don't have to tell me if you don't want to."

She turned to him and tilted her head as she looked at him. "My father is in a federal prison in Portland. He's been there since I was ten. My mother doesn't speak to me, only calls when I'm not home to leave a message, begging me to rethink the testimony I gave that put him there. You would think that she would have chosen to listen to her daughter once in the last seventeen years, but instead she sticks by him and his trail of lies."

"What happened?" He realized he was still hungry while she talked, so he finished his burger and reached in for a handful of fries, which were a little cold at this point, but still delicious.

"My father was part of a group of activists. He was caught with some plans which linked him to the murder of a twenty-four-year-old security guard at the nuclear power plant in Kalama, Washington. I'm the one that called the hotline. I'm the one that turned my father in." She turned to him, and he could see the tears in her blue eyes, turning them a lighter shade. "I watched him shoot the man in the face. He just pulled the gun out of his coat and shot him like it was nothing. Then he took his nine-year-old daughter out for bubblegum ice cream."

She turned back towards the water. "That weekend was my birthday, and I got to spend an extra hour watching cartoons. But instead I switched the television to the news channel. I saw the report about the murder, and they had a phone number at the bottom of the screen. I used my Mickey Mouse coloring book and my new crayons to write it down. Then later that day, I sneaked into the guest room and called it. At first they thought I was just some kid who'd dialed the wrong number." She laughed. "They kept hanging up on me. But by the third call, I finally blurted out that my daddy shot the man with curly blond hair in the face. That got their attention, since they hadn't released any details on how he'd died, other than he'd been shot. The police showed up an hour later, and I was taken into protective custody."

"Amber, I don't know what to say." He didn't. He'd thought he was going through some rough stuff, but to be all alone in the world and to feel the betrayal that she'd felt, he couldn't imagine it.

She looked at him and smiled. "Say that you won't tell a soul. I've moved around, running from it since that day. My mother pretty much left me alone the rest of my childhood. No more birthday parties, no more crayons, nothing. When I was seventeen I moved out, and I haven't seen her since. You were very lucky to have your grandparents. I can see in your grandmother's eyes that she would do anything for you."

He smiled. "Yeah, she would."

"Luke, I'm sorry your grandmother is sick. I can only imagine how much she means to you."

"You know what? We're a bunch of depressing people. Here we are sitting on a dock on a beautiful day, eating wonderful food, and all we can do is talk about sad and depressing things." He stood abruptly and held out his hand for hers. "I feel like having a piece of that chocolate pie." She set the nearly empty container of fries down and took his hand. When he pulled her up, he pulled her close. "Do you still have some time on your lunch break?"

She looked down at her watch. "Fifteen minutes left."

"Perfect. But not enough time to go back to your place, so what do you say to me buying you a big piece at the restaurant?"

"I'd say make it an apple pie and add a scoop of ice cream and you have yourself a deal."

"Mmm, that sounds even better." He picked up the container of fries and tossed them out for the birds, then dumped the trash in the trashcan. Then they walked back to the Golden Oar, hand in hand.

# Chapter Nine

By the time he got back home, he was in a better mood then he'd been in all month. When he arrived home he was greeted with laughter and wonderful smells. The four women were in the kitchen cooking. His gran sat in her wheelchair laughing, which caused him to smile.

"Well, there he is now. We were just wondering when you were going to be home. We're just getting ready for some company tonight. Your grandmother thought it would be nice to invite a few friends over."

His smile dropped away a little. "Gran? Are you going to be up to it?"

"Oh my, yes, dear. I think it's a lovely idea. I always wanted to say my goodbyes on my own terms. None of this hanging about until I look dreadful. I want everyone to see me while I'm still in my prime." She smiled, causing him to smile. Yup, that was his gran. Always doing things her own way. He thought it was a great idea.

"Well, naturally we've been in here cooking all day. We even made a batch of those brownies you love so much," one of the sisters said, causing him to look about the room quickly. "On, no. We have them tucked away. You can have some later. Now go clean up and wear something nice. Guests will be arriving soon."

He rushed from the room in hopes of getting his hands on a brownie early. By the time he was cleaned up and dressed in dark brown slacks and a green button-up shirt, he thought he heard more voices in the house. When he walked out, he saw the entire Jordan clan, Father Michael, Patty, several of the other church women, and a few other families his grandparents had been close to, all sitting or standing around.

"Good, you're here," Annie said, carrying a large plate of cheese and crackers in her hands. "You can help me fill drink orders."

He spent the next ten minutes getting everyone drinks. When he was done, he realized more people had entered. He was in the process of carrying several glasses into the living room when Amber walked in. She'd changed out of her uniform and was wearing a slick green dress that made him pause. She looked stunning. He was happy to see her there and immediately handed the drinks to someone and mumbled something about handing them out.

Then he was standing in front of her, and she was smiling at him. "You know; you'll never make any good tips that way."

"Huh? Oh! Yeah, well. I wasn't made to be on my feet ten hours out of the day." He smiled and took her hand. "You look wonderful." He leaned in. "And you smell wonderful, too." She laughed and pushed him lightly on the arm.

"It was so wonderful for your grandmother to invite me. She wasn't too clear about what the occasion is." She looked around the room at all the people.

"She's saying goodbye." His smile felt forced.

"Oh!" She looked at him. "Are you okay with this?"

He nodded. "You know, at first I was hesitant. But then I saw her smile and the peace in her eyes. She wants to do things her way. My grandfather didn't get to say goodbye to any of his family or friends. Who am I to tell her what she can and can't do? Besides, it's the happiest I've seen her in a while." He nodded to where his grandmother sat with one of Megan's kids on her lap. The little girl was gently looking at his gran's necklace, something he'd always seen her wear.

"She does look happy. How's she doing?"

"She has her moments. Today is a good day." He smiled and pulled her along the hallway towards the back room where he thought there were fewer people, but the room was just as packed. He wanted to be alone with her, but before he could figure out a place to go, Megan and Allison walked by, and before he knew what was happening, all three women walked off together, leaving him standing in the doorway alone.

He liked that Amber was friendly with all his friends' wives, but he really did want to get her alone. Over the next hour and a half, he spent his time talking to all of his friends, playfully chasing small kids around the house, and trying to get Amber alone for a few minutes.

When families with small children started leaving, he was relieved to finally get a chance to get Amber all alone. He'd seen her head down the long hallway towards the bathroom, and he'd stood at the end, waiting for her. When she walked out, he smoothly maneuvered her up the stairs and through his bedroom door. His gran had given him the master bedroom after his grandfather had died. She'd told him she didn't need all that empty space to herself. Plus, he knew she couldn't really maneuver the stairs well, so he actually had the whole upstairs of the house to himself. The master bedroom was huge, and spotless, thanks to his quick dash before everyone had started arriving.

She walked around his room looking at everything. "So, you like video games?" She turned towards him, and he could see the frown on her face.

If Amber needed any more proof that it was a bad idea to get involved with Luke, all she had to do was take one look at his room. Everything was covered with video game images. Posters hung on the wall in glass frames. There was a huge cutout of several figures in the corner of his room by the closet doors. A large desk with three of the largest computer screens she had ever seen sat on the far wall. The screen saver flashed images of game graphics, one after the other.

Yes, getting involved with Luke would end up just like her last few relationships. No more man-boys for her. When she turned to him he was smiling and walking towards her.

"Don't you like games?" The smile on his face told her he wasn't talking about computer games. Holding her hands up, she tried to ward him off.

"Sure, but there is a time and place for everything. I don't really enjoy sitting in front of the computer or television for hours playing a mindless game."

"Mindless, huh? Who says they're all mindless?"

"The last three guys I've dated are living proof that they are mindless." She backed up some more, still holding up her hands, as he continued to walk towards her.

"You dated three gamers in a row?" When she nodded, he continued. "Don't you know you're supposed to take a break between dating man-boys."

"Exactly!" Finally, someone got her. But then she looked around again and remembered he was one of those man-boys.

"Amber, I'm not like those other guys you've dated. This," he waved his hand around, motioning to his stuff, "is work. I suppose on some level it's pleasure as well. But for the most part it's how I make my living."

"Oh great. Another one of those." She felt defeated. He opened his mouth to speak, but just then there was a knock on his door.

"Yes?" He turned away from her.

"Oh, there you two are. Luke, your grandmother is a little tired and would like to lie down. Everyone else has left. Why don't you walk Amber home? We'd hate for her to walk all that way by herself."

He turned back towards her with a grin on his face. At that moment, she wanted nothing more than to walk home alone. She needed to clear her mind of Luke Crawford.

Five minutes later, Luke was helping her on with her coat. Even though the day had been warm, when she stepped out on the front deck she was thankful she'd brought her long wool coat and gloves. She'd walked the seven blocks to his house because she'd looked and seen all the cars parked up and down the town streets. Now, however, just his truck and his car were in the driveway.

"Are those sisters staying here?" she asked as they started walking. He'd put on his brown leather jacket and had grabbed her hand as he walked.

"Yeah. They've been my grandmother's best friends since they were children. It's sad none of them ever got married. I think they enjoy each other's company too much to let any men come between them."

She giggled. "I'd never seen triplets before. I've seen plenty of twins, but not three women who looked so much alike."

"I can tell you which one is Annie, but the other two?" He shook his head. "Not a clue."

She chuckled. His hand felt warm in hers, and she enjoyed the closeness of him. She kept trying to convince herself that he was just another bad decision. He told her stories of his childhood as they walked. Pointing out a large oak tree, he told her he'd had his first kiss leaning against it.

"She was two years older than me. A freshman in high school. I was so cool for having kissed a high school girl back then. The other guys worshiped me until Iian got to make out with Pam Steller in the back of his dad's car."

107

She chuckled as he continued to tell her about his neighbors. She knew most of the people still lived in town. He pointed to the houses along the way that had new families in them, all three of them. She was enchanted by how he told a story, painting a picture of the wonderful people around them.

By the time they made it to her place, she was having a hard time remembering that he was bad for her. He followed her up the stairs and she turned with her keys in hand to look at him. He stood a step below her which put them eye to eye. She could totally get lost in those copper eyes. She didn't realize that she'd leaned close to him until his arms wrapped around her waist and pulled her closer. She could smell the crisp night air and feel his warm breath on her face. She wanted more than anything to lean in for a kiss, knowing he could and would take her to places she enjoyed.

"I can see your mind working." He smiled at her. "What's holding you back?"

"Luke…" She placed her hands on his shoulders. "I've just come out of a bad relationship. You know my history. I just don't want to fall into the same pattern." She tried to pull away.

"I've told you. I don't spend hours and hours playing games. It's a job." He pulled her closer and buried his face in her neck. "You smell so good." He started nibbling on her neck and she closed her eyes, enjoying the feel of his hot mouth on her cooled skin. She moved her hands on his shoulders

108

until she was holding him to her instead of trying to push him away.

How could a man do this to her? She'd always stayed in control with the other men in her life. Sure, she'd fallen for some tricks here and there, but she didn't think Luke was trying to trick her now. His mouth traveled up her neck until he was kissing her, and she felt like her world was tilting. His hands moved from her hips to her back, rubbing circles under her coat. He pulled her closer until there wasn't a whisper of a breath between them. She felt his heart beat against hers and imagined what it would feel like to remove all the barriers.

She pulled back and looked at him, realizing she'd already crossed that line.

She knew he could see it in her face, because he took a deep breath and smiled. "You said something earlier today about having extra chocolate pie in your fridge?" He rested his forehead against hers as she chuckled.

"Yeah, how about I make us some coffee, and you can help me eat the rest of the pie?"

When she walked in, she rushed to the thermostat and upped the temperature.

"Why don't you leave that thing at a reasonable temperature? That way when you get home, the place is warm."

"It's wasteful. Besides, I enjoy feeling the place warm up. It's kinda like inching your way into a warm bath. You have to do it gradually."

"See, now you've got me thinking about you naked in a bath." He chuckled. "Go, make us some coffee and get that pie before I take you into the next room; we both know it's too soon for that."

She smiled and walked into the next room. Okay, so she had to give him props for being open and honest, something no other man had ever been with her. After all, he'd shared his whole life experience with her. She'd even broken her cardinal rule and told him about her family. She'd never done that with another man before.

When she walked into the living room a few minutes later, he was standing by the windows.

"You know; I never get used to how beautiful this town is during the holidays. I mean, look at it." He waved his hand.

A few days back, a group of people had come and hung up white lights over Main Street. At night they lit up so that she didn't even have to turn on her living room lights anymore. Instead the warm glow from the street lit up the room. Wreathes hung on every street light. There were small flags with turkeys on them that said Happy Thanksgiving. They had replaced the ones that had a jack-o-lantern for Halloween.

She supposed they would put the Christmas ones up the day after Thanksgiving. Maybe even add more lights here and there.

"Do they do a community Christmas tree?" she asked as she handed him a plate with a large piece of pie. She set his coffee cup down on her coffee table.

"Yeah, they put it up in the main square, across from the library and town hall." He pointed to the left. "It's something to see." He turned and she watched him take a bite of the pie.

"Chocolate, huh?" She smiled.

"What?" He licked a dab of chocolate off his bottom lip. She followed his tongue's motion, dreaming.

"Chocolate. You're a chocoholic, I think." She smiled at him.

"Isn't everyone?"

"No, some people enjoy it, some people can't stand it, but you...every time chocolate is mentioned, your eyes light up and you get this goofy look that crosses your face."

She laughed as he made the face. "Yes, that's it."

He laughed, too. "Yeah, it's my kryptonite. Anytime I didn't want to do something growing up, my grandmother would just bake a batch of her brownies, and she'd have a slave."

"I'm surprised you don't weigh more." She laughed and took a bite of the pie. She'd been eating it all week long, but each bite was like heaven.

"Yeah, well, you can thank those weekly basketball games. I've got to stay in shape if I don't want to get myself killed. It's murder playing with that bunch. You should stop by sometime and watch a game. Some days we have a whole crowd there. Megan, Lacey, Allison, and the kids come every now and then."

"I've always liked watching basketball. My favorite sport to watch is hockey, though. There's just something about a bunch of big guys in padding, beating each other up." She grinned.

"Well, if you like watching that, you will definitely enjoy watching a bunch of sweaty guys, half of us shirtless, knocking each other around. Why do you think Megan, Lacey, and Allison make a point to show up?" They both laughed.

# Chapter Ten

Less than a week later, Amber received another call from her mother. This time she sounded more urgent.

"Amber, I know you don't care too much about me, but maybe you'd think about your father for a change. His health is failing inside the prison, and all he wants is to be free. He has thirty more years on his sentence and this appeal is the only hope he has of getting out early. Give Mr. Malone a call, or I'll give him your direct number."

The message machine clicked. She felt like picking up the machine and tossing it across the room. There was no way her father was going to walk out of prison early because of her. If she showed up at all, she would make sure they kept him in that cell until the very second his heart stopped. She wasn't cold hearted, but after seeing how two-faced her dad was, she doubted he'd ever feel remorse for the crime. After all, according to him, the guard had deserved it because he worked for a company that was killing the earth.

Sure, she was somewhat of a nature lover herself. But there was no way she'd ever condone anything like what her father and his group had been planning. The plans had just been a small part of the operation. When the investigators had found her father's friends, they'd found a large cache of bomb material. Apparently their goal was to blow up the main power facilities in Portland and Seattle, hitting both places in one night. They would have killed thousands of people, all in the name of saving the planet.

She decided it was early enough to head down to the market to finish getting the things on her shopping list. She knew she needed to take a trip into Edgeview soon. So far she'd traveled the twenty-minute drive a few times. She enjoyed the winding ocean roads and liked Edgeview enough. They had a Walmart and other major stores where she could easily find what she needed.

But for tonight she just headed downstairs, feeling a little more worn out after listening to her mother's message.

When she walked in, she wished she'd waited five more minutes. There at the checkout stood Patty, chatting happily away with Ruth.

When she walked in, the two of them quieted down and looked at her oddly. She grabbed a basket and started down the closest aisle. When she

114

reached the back of the aisle, she heard them chatting again. Closing her eyes and taking a deep breath, she tried to focus on her shopping. When she had a full basket, she walked to the front with her head down, looking at the items, mentally checking if she'd gotten everything.

She didn't realized Ruth was still standing in the same spot until she almost bumped into her.

"Oh, I'm sorry. I guess I need to watch where I'm going. Don't you hate it when you think you've forgotten something?" She set her basket down and started emptying the contents onto the conveyer belt.

"Yes, well." Ruth stood aside. "I was in Eugene last weekend, visiting my son. He and his wife have lived there for the last ten years. They have four of the best children. Anyway, I remembered that your mother lives there and decided to stop by for a quick visit."

Amber could hear her heartbeat in her ears, and felt all the blood leave her face and hands.

"Anyway, it had been some time since I'd visited Donna. I'd say about sixteen years. Of course the second I saw her again I remembered you as a little girl. Lone children can be so spoiled sometimes. That's why my Edward has four. Anyway..."

At this point Amber wished to be anywhere but where she was. She looked around frantically for someone, anyone to help her excuse herself. There

115

was no one else inside the store this late at night except the three of them.

"Anyway..." Ruth repeated. "Your mother told me the story of how your father was incarcerated, all because you told a fib."

There it was. The ugly lie had spread. There was no way she'd ever feel welcome in this town again. She was finding it hard to breathe. Her vision grayed around the edges and she knew, just knew, that at any moment she would hit the floor.

"Well, I want you to know I stood up right there in her florescent pink living room, set my tea cup down, and said in a clear voice, 'There is no way the Amber Kennedy I've met would ever lie about something so important. If she says that Frank Kennedy shot and killed that man seventeen years ago, then I believe her.' Then I told her that Frank Kennedy had always been a bad seed. I remember him in high school. That's where I know your parents from, by the way. Frank was always getting into trouble. Mouthing off, finding some good reason to do something stupid. Well..." Ruth took a deep breath. "I'll have you know your mother kicked me out of her house and told me to never come back."

"Good riddance, if you ask me," Patty said with a huff. "We sure are proud of you for standing up for what's right. You've earned your spot in this town, working as hard as you do down there at the Jordan's restaurant. Best manager they've had, besides Lacey, that is." The two women smiled and nodded.

"You don't worry yourself about that appeal coming up. If your mother is pestering you about it, you just tell her to give me a call, and I'll set her straight."

Amber was standing still, unsure about what had just happened. Surely these two strangers hadn't stood up for her? No one had ever stood up for her before. Not like this. She blinked a few times. When she opened her mouth, nothing came out.

"Oh, see what we've done. We've upset her now." Patty pulled out a box of tissues from behind her counter and handed a few to Amber. She looked down at them, unsure what to do. Then a tear hit her hand, and she realized she was crying.

"I'm sorry, Amber. I didn't mean to upset you. I just wanted you to hear the details of my visit from me and not your mother."

"It's just that...Well...I'm sorry." She wiped her eyes and face.

"It's okay, honey. I'm sorry we brought the whole subject up. Now we're standing around watching your ice cream melt," Patty said as she started to scan Amber's items quickly. Ruth helped her bag the items.

"Thank you, both of you. I'm sorry you found out about my past. I tried to hide it, and now I wish I would have come clean right away."

"Don't worry about it. We understand. We know we can be quite the gossips, but we both wanted you to know that your story wouldn't go any further than us. Some other people in town might not understand, since they don't know you like we do." They both shook their heads. "Well, we'll just keep it to ourselves. You tell whomever you want, whenever you feel more comfortable."

When Amber made it back upstairs, she realized her heart felt lighter than when she'd gone downstairs. Now she thought she could get through the night without downing the entire container of mint chocolate chip ice cream.

Luke's grandmother died in her sleep on the tenth of November, five days after her farewell party. She was seventy-nine years old. She'd looked at peace when he'd found her that morning. He'd instantly known when he'd entered her room that she wasn't there anymore. He'd walked over to her bed and sat on the edge, looking down at her in the dark room.

An hour later, when one of the Henderson sisters walked in, all his tears had been shed, or so he'd thought. It took a day to make all the final arrangements. His grandmother had set everything up for her funeral shortly after his grandfather had died. A steady stream of people came and went at all hours of the day, and the place always smelled of home cooking.

That first night was the hardest on him. Iian stayed until late. He'd even tried to crash on the couch, but Luke knew he needed to get home to Allison and their son, Conner. Finally, around midnight, he convinced him to leave. Luke walked down the hallway and looked into his grandma's dark room. He could still smell the fancy perfume he'd bought her for her last birthday. He knew the bottle sat on her dresser, a cherished prize she'd enjoyed.

Her funeral was all set for two days from now. No doubt the house would be packed with every member of the town afterwards. He knew he needed his sleep, but instead found himself up all night staring at the computer screen. Programming and designing helped take his mind off of how empty the house now felt.

He'd never realized how much his grandmother had filled the place with her smile, her laughter. When morning came around, he decided to take a quick drive and ended up at the old cemetery adjacent to the church. He knew he would be here again tomorrow, but he just needed to talk to his grandfather beforehand.

As he stood on the hill, looking down over the small, peaceful town, he could almost believe everything would be alright. He talked to his grandfather, knowing the good it did was only for him. He was thankful they hadn't started digging the grave yet for his gran. The grass next to his grandfather's marker was still green and whole. The night's rain had soaked the ground, and his boots sank a little in the grass as he chatted to himself.

He must have been standing there for an hour when he heard a cough behind him. Turning, he nodded to Father Michael.

"Hey." Luke stuck his hands in his coat pocket. He hadn't realized how cold he was until his fingers started tingling.

"How are you doing, son?" The father walked over and stood next to him, looking out across the cemetery towards the town.

"I'm hanging in there." Luke knew and liked the father. He'd been a steady staple in his life since they day he'd arrived in town as a lost child. Realizing he now felt a lot like that little boy so many years ago did little for his ego.

"I know it's hard to believe, but your grandmother is with your grandfather now, and most likely getting a warm welcome in heaven."

He smiled. "Yeah, but it doesn't make the hurt and loneliness go away." He turned to the father. "How does someone recover from losing everyone they've ever cared about? First my parents, now my second parents."

The father turned and looked at him. "Did you know I had a son? He'd be about your age, if he'd lived. When I was twenty-seven, he and my wife boarded a plane to visit my wife's family out east. The plane slid off the runway in Philly. I remember thinking the same thing back then. I'd come up here one day to pray and the priest, Father Patrick, had walked with me out here. He waved his hand over the view here." Father Michael waved his arm towards the hillside, the trees, and the town. "He told me, *'You have what you need in life. God never takes something without giving something else to help you.'*" Father Michael turned to Luke. "Then he said, *'You have Pride. Let the people here be your family. I can't take away your pain, your loneliness, but these people can and will.'*" The father put his arm around Luke's shoulder. "There isn't a day that goes by that I don't miss my old life. But there isn't a day that goes by that I'm not thankful for the people I love and surround myself with. They are the reason I wake up every day. The reason I do what I do and enjoy my job." He wiped a tear from his eyes. "Now, don't be going around saying that to anyone. As far as they know, God is the reason I do everything, and He is, because He gave me them." He waved his arm again, pointing to the small town.

Luke smiled, looking out over the town. He could see the smoke from the chimneys and the cars driving down the roads. He could even make out someone walking down the street in a bright red raincoat. He knew almost everyone in town. He liked every single person and loved living in Pride and couldn't imagine living anyplace else. He'd never given any thought to what he would do after his grandmother passed—would he stay here; would he go back east? —but somehow he'd always known he'd stay.

He knew that his gran's will ensured that almost everything went to him. There were a few items that went to his uncle and cousin in Portland, but the house was his.

He closed his eyes and took a deep breath, then turned to the Father and smiled. "How is it that you always say the right things? I can see that God gave us you in return." He shook the man's hand. "I knew that losing gran was going to be hard, but I had lost sight of everything I still had. Thank you."

# Chapter Eleven

Amber balanced the tray on her shoulder and tried not to notice that Luke was sitting in the large back room, surrounded by most of the people in town. Iian had shown up that morning and called her into his office. Today was Luke's grandmother's funeral, and instead of the whole town going to Luke's place, Iian wanted to host the party here, in the large back room. Amber had called all the staff and asked for everyone to come in and help out. Now the place was packed. Not just the back room, but the whole restaurant.

She'd seen Luke come in surrounded by his friends. He'd stood next to a man who could have been his twin, and she'd realized it must be his cousin Blake whom he'd talked about. The older man next to them was most likely his uncle. Iian kept close to his friend as well. The small kids

123

played, running around the back room as the adults chatted.

She'd made a decision to run the event as a buffet, and had ordered the chefs to make large amounts of some of their more popular dishes. She'd spent almost an hour setting up the long tables with some of the staff. The tables were lined up along the back wall and had large pans with gas burners keeping everything warm. A line was formed and everyone made it through quickly and smoothly and now sat at tables throughout the restaurant. Drinks were provided and desserts served and by the time the last guests left the place, Amber's feet hurt, and she'd worked herself into a small stress headache.

She hadn't had any time to stop by and talk privately to Luke. She felt bad and made a mental note to stop by that next day. Walking into her place, she decided a hot shower and some hot cocoa was in order. There was a new movie in her Netflix queue that she'd decided to watch, and she had a bag of caramel popcorn tucked away.

She was just about to get out of the bath when she heard the knocking on her door. Grabbing her thick pink robe, she went to the door, but when she opened it, no one was there. Poking her head out, she looked down the stairs and saw Luke's back as he headed down the stairs.

"Luke?" He turned when he heard her and started heading back up the stairs.

"I didn't know if you were..." He dropped away when he got to the top stair and noticed her standing there, dripping wet in her robe.

"Home?" she added for him, smiling a little. "Come on in, you're getting soaked." She pulled him inside by his coat front until he stood just inside her door, dripping on her mat. "You're soaked. How long did you stand out there knocking?" He pulled his jacket off and hung it to dry on her coat rack.

"I... I walked over." His eyes followed her every move.

"You walked? In this downpour?" She pointed to the large windows. Everything beyond the glass was gray and dark. The water slid down the outside of the glass.

"Yeah, well, when I started walking it wasn't raining."

She thought about it. It had been raining when she'd left work almost an hour ago. "You've been out in the weather for over an hour? Come in, sit down. No!" She realized that he was indeed soaking wet. "Hang on." She rushed to the bathroom, coming out with three large towels. Laying them on the couch, she motioned for him to sit. "If you want, I can stick your clothes in the dryer. I think I have an old pair of Chris' sweats around." She started to walk back to her room.

"No, that's okay. I'll be fine." She looked at him and realized he looked so lost. His hair was dripping in his face. He took one of the towels and dried his face and hair, and she watched his motions.

"I didn't mean to interrupt your...bath?"

"Yes." She nodded her head. "That's okay, I was getting out anyway. I'd been in too long, and I was starting to prune up." She waved her fingers at him. "I didn't get a chance to talk to you today. I'm sorry about your grandmother. I only met her that once, but she was a sweet woman."

He smiled. "She couldn't stop talking about you after that night." He sat there looking at her. She looked down and realized she was still in her robe.

"Oh, um...If you'll give me a minute, I'll go change."

He nodded his head, and she disappeared into her room to change. Running into her bathroom, she towel-dried her hair and ran a comb through it. She knew it would dry quickly. She opted to put on an old pair of jeans and a large comfortable red sweater. She put on her thick socks and dabbed a bit of her favorite perfume behind her ears.

Checking her reflection, she wished she could take a little time to apply make-up, but knew she'd kept him waiting long enough.

When she walked out, he was standing by the windows, looking out at the dark street. The rain had let up a little. When she walked over, she noticed the streets were flooded, the drains strained from all the water rushing down the streets.

"You know, I never realized what a great view you have here. Somehow looking down at Main Street is soothing."

She smiled, realizing she'd thought the same thing. "I enjoy standing here in the mornings. It's fun to watch people rushing about, getting their business done."

He turned to look at her. He'd removed his wet sweatshirt and his white t-shirt was fairly dry.

"I can see why people stay here their whole lives. It's more than just the view and the location. It's the people. My grandparents moved here shortly after my uncle was born. When both of their boys decided to leave after high school, they stayed. Then after I graduated, I went to school out east. But I returned when my grandfather died, and now..." He looked back out to the street.

Her heart did a little dip. She'd never once thought that he'd been staying in Pride due to his grandmother. If he left, she'd feel a small empty spot. The realization of it caught her off guard. She turned her head back to the window and thought about what it all meant.

She knew she'd been telling herself that he was just another man-child. For all she knew, he did stay up all night playing video games. After all, his room was decorated in early teen fashion.

"I can't really imagine leaving here." He turned back to her. "Why does it seem like I keep ending up at your place? Burdening you."

127

She looked at him. His copper eyes looked a little dull, and she remembered how he'd looked at the dinner. Making up her mind, she smiled at him. "You're not a burden. Actually, you are just what I needed. A big strong man to save me from the werewolves."

He smiled and looked around. "Werewolves? I don't see any werewolves."

"Oh, but you will." She walked over and turned on her television. "You see, I was too busy to watch this for Halloween, so I've saved it especially for a spooky, rainy night when some tall, dark, handsome stranger would come knocking on my door to protect me."

She motioned to the couch. When he just looked at her like she was losing it, she piped in, "I'll make hot chocolate and caramel corn."

He smiled and sat down, crossing his foot over his knee. "Well?" He motioned to the television. "Let's get this party started."

He didn't know how she could say that she'd watched the movie. After all, her eyes were covered for over half the movie. He'd sat there with her tucked close to his side, and at some points she was almost in his lap. She'd squealed at every scary moment and had covered her ears and eyes when the music would build before a scary scene. He laughed and loved every minute. At one point she had even spilled a little hot chocolate on him when a dog had jumped out of a dark alley on the screen. She'd made a bag of caramel popcorn; it had been years since he'd had caramel popcorn.

By the end of the movie, he felt like his old self. He'd smiled, laughed, and even at one point, been a little scared himself.

"Well, I can see why the movie made so much money at the box office. It's been a while since I went to a movie at a theater."

"I expect so, since they don't have one in Edgeview. Do you know, that was the second thing I checked out when I drove through there?"

"Really? What was the first?"

"To see if they had a Starbucks. I can't believe there isn't a coffee shop in town."

He shook his head. "Yeah, the coffee Patty gives out for free to customers just can't compare to a cappuccino." He laughed.

She chuckled, "Do you know, the first time she offered me a cup, I drank it and had to force myself to swallow it all and not spit it out. I didn't want to hurt her feelings."

They were sitting on her couch, pretty much in the same position that they'd been during the movie, but it felt more intimate now that the television was black. His arm was slung over her shoulders and it was the most natural thing to lean over and place a soft kiss on her lips.

She tasted like caramel and smelled like sin. His hands moved around her neck and into her soft hair. He could still feel a few damp strands in her hair from her bath. Her skin was soft and smooth as he ran his other hand over her neck, pulling the large sweater to the side, exposing her neck. His lips left hers, running a trail down her slender neck. Here he found more of the sinful smell which had driven him nuts during the movie. He licked her slowly behind the ear and felt her shiver under his hands. Then she moaned and wrapped her fingers in his hair, holding him to her.

"Luke," she moaned. He pulled back and looked at her. Her blue eyes were closed, and her head was leaning back against the back of the couch. Using one finger, he softly moved her sweater until the large open neckline fell off her bare shoulder. He wondered if she wore anything on under it. Her eyes opened and he could see desire; her blue eyes were unfocused and cloudy with want. He leaned in and took her mouth again as her hands reached for him.

She was half on his lap, so he pulled her up until she straddled him. Her hands continued to hold onto his hair, but when he moved to run his hands over her hips, she lowered her hands to his shoulders. She ran her hands over his arms, and he moaned at the feel of her light touch.

Slowly he moved his hands up until he felt her skin under her sweater. Her hands followed his hint, but instead of going slow, she reached for the bottom of his shirt and pulled until it came loose, so she could pull it up and off him.

"Mmm, I just love the look of you." She leaned down and placed soft kisses on his neck, running her hot mouth down to his chest.

He was floored. His hands held her hips in place as she tortured him. When her mouth traveled back to his, he pulled on her sweater until she leaned back and smiled at him. Then he helped her slowly lift the ends until she exposed inch by soft inch of her skin. His fingers touched her skin as he went, his eyes on hers.

When she stopped, just before pulling it all the way off, his heart skipped a beat. Then she smiled and allowed him to pull it the rest of the way off. He'd been right, she was bare underneath.

"Beautiful," he murmured as he leaned up to taste her perfect skin. Her head fell back, and her hands went to hold him next to her. He lost himself in pleasing them both. As he slowly trailed his mouth over every inch of her, his hands traveled, feeling every inch of her perfect little body. He had to have more, but knew he wanted to go slow, to enjoy every moment.

"Luke, please." She took his face in her hands and placed a soft kiss on his lips.

"Amber, I just..." He couldn't explain it. He knew he wanted this to be special. Needed it to be.

131

He leaned his forehead on hers and took a deep breath. "Maybe this isn't such a good idea."

She moved back like she'd been splashed with cold water. He pulled her closer. "No, don't. Listen. I'm just..." He closed his eyes and leaned his head back against the couch. How could he explain to her that he was screwed up right now? He didn't want this to be about him, which it would be if they continued. It had been a while, seven months, since he'd been with anyone. It wasn't as if he felt like he could control himself around her. Not now, when his emotions were so raw.

When he opened his eyes up, he saw understanding in her blue eyes. He took her face in his hands and kissed her softly. "Thank you for understanding."

She insisted on driving him the short distance back to his place. The rain had let up a little, but not much, so he was happy to be in out of the cold. When he walked into the place, he realized how truly empty it was. Well, he could do something about that, just not tonight.

He went up to his room and slept all the way through the night. The next morning, he woke up and made French toast, something his gran had taught him, but he hadn't made in a long while. The house smelled better and even felt a little warmer. He took his time cleaning the kitchen, putting the dishes away and making sure everything shined like it was supposed to. Then he put on his snow boots, since he had that feeling in his bones, and grabbed his keys.

An hour later, he walked back in with a new friend who spent the next hour sniffing everything and dribbling pee puddles, which he quickly mopped up.

It wasn't the first puppy to live in this house. Actually, that's one of the main reasons the whole downstairs had hardwood floors. When he was eleven he'd talked his grandfather into getting a basset hound. Butch had quickly learned the rules of the house and had lived to the ripe old age of eleven before finally falling to sleep for the last time one day behind the shed.

Looking down at the small female beagle, he started running through names while he made himself a sandwich for lunch. He knew he needed a quick run to the store to grab the necessities: a dog bed, leash, flea collar, and other items he thought of.

He'd gone through about a hundred names when it came to him. Jackie. Actually, it had been thanks to a John Mellencamp song that had been playing on the radio as he'd driven her home. Since she was a girl, he couldn't call her Jack, and he didn't like the name Diane. He liked Jackie, and even thought he could get away with calling her Jack some of the time.

"Well, Jackie. What do you think?" The puppy sat down on her little bottom, her tail wagging as her tongue lolled about. He'd grabbed a small bag of the food the vet had recommended, but he wanted to run to Patty's and pick up a large bag of the food that they had always given Butch.

An hour later, with Jackie safely tucked in the laundry room with a warm towel to snuggle up to, he trudged through the falling snow towards Patty's.

When he arrived, he noticed that people instantly put on their "sad" faces. He tried to ignore it as he filled his cart with every item he wanted in the pet aisle.

"Oh, did you get a puppy?" Patty asked as he pulled his cart to the checkout stand.

"Yes, a beagle, this morning."

"Oh, how precious. One from Becky and Tom's litter?"

He nodded. "A girl. I've named her Jackie."

"How sweet." Patty smiled as she scanned all the items. "Going to spoil her rotten." She chuckled when she scanned a large bag of treats.

Just then the door chime rang. When he looked up he saw Amber, who looked a little flushed as she noticed him at the checkout. Her steps faltered a little as she walked over to grab a cart.

Of course Patty noticed it, and he could have sworn that her smile got bigger. He actually heard her humming as she continued to scan his items. When everything was in bags, Patty continued to talk to him about the puppy until finally Amber stood behind him with a half-full cart.

"Did you hear that Luke just got a puppy?" Patty smiled and looked pleased with herself.

"You got a puppy? Oh. What kind?"

He chuckled, and told her the story. By the end of the conversation, he had somehow been maneuvered by Patty into helping Amber drop off her groceries and then taking her back up to his place to show her Jackie.

When Amber opened her door, she turned back around. "How is it that woman can talk anyone into doing what she suggests?"

He chuckled. "I know what you mean. When she sets her mind on something, it usually happens." He carried her bags into the kitchen. "Listen, if you don't want to come over to see Jackie, you don't have to."

"Nonsense." Amber stopped in the process of putting a bag of powdered sugar away. "I'm actually dying to see your new little girl." She smiled and turned back around.

He started pulling items out of the bag. "Okay, I just didn't want you to feel weird."

She stopped and turned back to him. "Weird?"

"Yeah, well...you know. When you entered the store, it looked like you were about to turn around and run out the door when you saw me."

She paled a little. "Oh, that was nothing." She turned back around and started putting her groceries away. He set a can of tomato soup down and walked over to her, cornering her against the counter top.

When she turned back around, he placed his hands on her hips to hold her still. "It's not nothing. Why do I get the idea you're trying to brush me off?"

He could see her make up her mind. "I'm not ready for a relationship just now. I keep telling myself that, but then when I'm around you, you're so easy to get along with. More so than anyone else I've ever seen on a personal level. It's so hard for me to step back."

"Then don't. Listen, Amber, I'm not asking for your hand in marriage. I'm not at that place in my life just yet. I don't think we know each other well enough at this point. But I do think we have something between us, and I want to explore it, and I think you do as well."

She nodded her head. "Good, so what do you say to finishing this up, then heading back to my place to play with a puppy? Then, if you're good, I might just make you dinner." He wiggled his eyebrows.

# Chapter Twelve

Amber laughed again as the puppy tried to crawl up the front of her shirt and kiss her on the lips.

"She knows how sweet tasting your mouth is." Luke chuckled from his position leaning against the countertop.

"She's the most precious thing I've ever seen. I've never had a puppy before. I always wanted one, or a pony." She laughed again when the puppy managed to get a good lick on her chin.

"Yeah, well, puppies are a lot easier to clean up after. Which reminds me, it's about time to go out." He opened the kitchen door that led to the backyard. The puppy climbed off her lap, falling on her face, but quickly picked herself up and trotted out the door.

"Oh, aren't you suppose to go out with her? Watch her or something?" Concern had her up and to the door as he laughed at her.

"No, I think she can handle it on her own."

"Oh, but what about birds, or foxes?"

"There aren't any foxes in my backyard. As for birds, I think they are more afraid of Jack than she is of them."

"Not those kinds of birds. Hawks or eagles. Don't they eat small animals like her?"

"Well..." She didn't hear anything else he had to say, she was out the back door and looking around for the small helpless dog.

Luke stood in the back doorway and smiled as she hunted the large backyard for the small dog. Finally, she spotted her behind the shed. When she walked over there, the puppy looked up at her as she was doing her business. She could have sworn she looked embarrassed to be caught, causing Amber to chuckle. Amber quickly turned her back and apologized.

"Did you just apologize to my dog for catching her going to the bathroom?"

"Yes, we ladies need our privacy." Jackie walked up behind her and started sniffing her shoes. "There." Amber bent to pick her up. "All is forgiven." She walked across the yard, holding the dog.

"She can walk you know." He laughed.

"Oh, I know. But we don't want to get all muddy, do we, Jackie?" She snuggled and kissed the puppy on the forehead.

"And Patty thought I was going to spoil her."

"What?" Amber looked up at him with innocent eyes.

He laughed. "Nothing."

The rain had finally let up, but his backyard was still muddy and when she walked by him, she slipped a little on the grass. His arm reached out to hold her steady, and she felt a jolt of pure lust rush through her system.

How did he do that to her? One minute she was kissing puppies, and the next she was imagining them naked.

She'd been doing the same thing when she'd entered the store earlier. Actually, that had been the cause of her face turning red when she'd seen him.

She couldn't help it, he looked so damn sexy in his faded jeans and leather jacket. He'd been wearing a ball cap today, and she'd found it very appealing. To be honest, she was glad for the opportunity to visit again. She'd enjoyed their time last night and wanted to see if she felt the same way about him in daylight. She did. Now she knew she had two paths to go: either keep denying it and slowly pull away, denying her needs, or go for it and see where the road took her. If it ended up in hurt and pain, so be it. It wasn't as if she hadn't taken that road before.

"Okay, are you done figuring it out?" He smiled down at her. Jackie was squirming between them. He pulled back and took the small puppy from her arms, setting it gently down in the grass. Then she was back in his arms.

"Yes, I think so." She smiled at him. "Have you?"

His smile faded a little, and he shook his head no. "I'm not sure." Then he smiled. "But I do like it when you try to persuade me." She wrapped her arms around his neck as he pulled her closer. Then he leaned in and took her mouth.

The cold breeze blew between them, causing her to inch closer to his warmth. He had a way of using his mouth on her that made her legs melt.

His hands were in her hair again, and she realized hers were in his. He moved his slowly down her neck and shoulders until he was making small circles on her back and hips. She couldn't get over how nice his muscles felt under her fingertips. When she started shaking with want, he pulled back.

"How about I make you some food?"

She smiled and nodded. "That sounds wonderful. That is, if you can cook." She frowned a little. "I guess I should have asked you that before agreeing to eat here."

He laughed. "Yes, my gran taught me well. And after all, my best friend is a chef. What do you say to some steaks and shrimp cocktail?"

"Yum!"

Amber was impressed at the way Luke moved around the kitchen like a pro. She was even more impressed when she tasted the delicious-smelling food.

"Wow. Just wow. Does Iian know you cook like this?" She took another mouthwatering bite.

"Yes. Actually, he taught me how to fix the shrimp just right." He laughed. "He keeps trying to get me to fill in down at the restaurant, but it's not for me."

"No, I suppose not." She looked at her plate, remembering his room full of games.

"Yeah, I know that tone. The last two girls I dated had that same tone. You really will have to see what I do to believe it. Just trust me, I don't play video games all night." He smiled.

She nodded her head. She hadn't meant to bring up his employment. Honestly, she tried to keep it out of their conversations.

"I'm sure you don't." She tried to change the subject by bringing up Jackie again, only to have him laugh at her attempt.

"Fine, we won't talk about my job. One day you will find out exactly what it is I do, though. For

141

now, I'll leave it alone. So, tell me, who is the worse waitress down at the restaurant? I bet its Arleen. The old girl has been around since Iian's grandfather ran the place."

She laughed.

When Amber made it back to her place, for the first time in years she felt lonely. She was jealous of Luke's ability to have a puppy. Living in apartments for a big chunk of her life, she'd never been able to have pets. She couldn't have cats, since she had a mild allergy.

Maybe she'd look around and see about buying or renting a house so she could get a puppy. She thought about the small bundle and started planning.

The weeks before Thanksgiving flew by. They decorated the restaurant, changing some of the basic items to more holiday-oriented items. She had been working up her nerve to bring up a few suggestions she had to Iian. When she finally did work up the nerve to step into his office, he was sitting behind the desk, and Luke sat beside him with his feet up on Iian's desk. They were both laughing.

She wanted to turn back around and run. She'd seen Luke again on several occasions, each one ending with a heavy make-out and petting session, but ending with that. She was getting frustrated and wanted badly to just jump his bones. But she understood he was going through an emotionally hard time, so she stepped back each time.

She wasn't usually one to take that first step, but with him she couldn't seem to stop herself.

"Amber, come on in," Luke said, smiling as if he had a secret.

"Well, if this is a bad time..." She looked towards Iian, making sure to say it so he could read her lips.

"No, I have a few minutes. I'm about to head out. Actually, you know what. Why don't you come with us?" Iian stood and smiled at his friend. "It's game day and we're playing the Hornets, the boys and girls basketball team, today. We could use the extra cheering."

"What?" She stepped back, her back came up against the door. "No, I can't—"

Iian waved at her. "Please, I have it on good authority that your boss won't mind. Besides, it's a slow day, and Thomas can take over for a few hours."

"I..." She searched Iian's and Luke's faces for an excuse. Coming up with none, she sighed.

"Good!" Iian smiled. "Luke, you can drive her over to the gym. I'll see you both there." Iian walked out, whistling, something he did often. Amber had been very impressed when she not only recognized the song, but found that he was in perfect tone.

Looking over to Luke she smiled. "Why does it seem the whole town has it out for us?"

143

He laughed. "Probably because they do. You should have seen it when everyone was trying to get Iian and Allison together." He laughed. "Come on, let's get going. The Hornets are a rough bunch and don't like us being late."

When they walked into the gym, Amber was happy to see Allison, Megan, a very pregnant Lacey, and another woman, with jet black curly hair, pale milky white skin, and deep red lips, sitting on the bleachers. Waving, she looked at Luke.

"Go ahead, sit with them. But make sure you cheer for me." He leaned over and kissed her quickly right in front of everyone. Smiling, he turned and walked into the changing rooms with his bag slung over his shoulder.

When she walked over to the bleachers, everyone said hello.

"Amber, this is Sara Lauren. She's just moved back into town from Seattle. We went to school together." Allison motioned to the dark-haired woman sitting next to her.

"Hello." Amber sat next to Megan. "Nice to meet you. Are you back to stay?"

"Yes. Sometimes you just wake up and know it's time to get out of the city." Sara smiled.

"I know what you mean." Then Amber turned to Megan and asked, "No kids today?"

"No, we decided to let Betty watch them at Lacey's so we can focus on cheering." Megan smiled.

Then Amber turned towards Lacey. "I can't believe they let you out of the house. Aren't you due any minute?"

"Yesterday." Lacey said. "I was due yesterday. I told Aaron that if I don't have this kid by tonight, he's going to have to induce. There is no way I'm waiting too much longer."

Amber smiled. "Well, you look wonderful."

"Bull, but thank you for saying so." Lacey smiled.

"Oh! Look, here they come." Megan stood and started cheering. The other ladies followed along.

Amber watched as eight grown men came running out of the locker rooms, all wearing green jerseys with the name "Sasquatch" on the front. She laughed.

"Yeah, their idea." Megan laughed along, clapping as the men ran in circles, tossing a basketball back and forth.

"Who's that?" Sara pointed to Allen.

"Oh, that's right. You haven't met the new hunk," Allison said over her shoulder. "He's the head of the coast guard that just moved in down the road. They've just opened a unit in the old saw mill. They plan on having a helicopter and a base out of Pride.

Allen's spent the last year overseeing the operation. He's going to be training all the new recruits. I guess he's some fancy pilot, too."

"Hmm," Sara said with a sparkle in her eyes.

"Yeah. Hmmm." All the women chuckled in unison. Even the very pregnant Lacey.

Then, from the other side of the gym, a group of thirteen and fourteen-year-olds came running out of the opposite lockers. They all had yellow jerseys that said Hornets on the front.

"They're playing teenagers?" Amber asked as she clapped.

"Yeah, they're vicious," Megan said, still watching her husband jog around the court. "Of course it doesn't help that our boys have to play by the rules," Megan said this as two referees walked out of the lockers. "The Hornets never play by the rules." She smiled at Amber.

Thirty minutes later, Amber realized the Sasquatches were in trouble. They were down five points. The kids looked like they could continue running up and down the court endlessly, while the men were beginning to look a little winded.

They were five minutes into the second half when Lacey squealed and a gush of fluid rushed out from under her skirt. Amber freaked. Megan and Allison smiled and cheered. Sara stood there wondering what was going, a look on her face much like the one on Amber's face. Aaron rushed over to his wife, interrupting the game.

Ten minutes later, with the game canceled on account of a new baby, Amber stood around waiting for her ride back to the restaurant as Luke showered. She'd talked to Sara for a few minutes before she'd left and was excited to have met someone else who had recently moved into town, even though Sara had lived here before.

"Hey," Luke said, walking out of the locker room with his bag slung over his shoulder. "Sorry it took so long. Those kids really hog up the hot water." He walked up and took her hand in his as they started walking towards the door. "How about we swing by the restaurant and grab some dinner?"

She smiled and thought she'd give him one more chance. "How about we stop by my place? That is, if Jackie will be okay by herself? I can cook you dinner."

"Sounds good. Jackie is a big girl and tucked away nicely in the laundry room with plenty of food, water, and newspaper. You don't have to go back to work?" He opened the truck door for her.

"No, I had just clocked out when I walked into Iian's office." She hit her head with her hand. "Which reminds me, I didn't get a chance to talk to him about the changes."

"What changes?" Luke walked around and got in the truck.

"I've been thinking about talking to Iian about some of the ideas I've had to change the place up a little."

"Yeah? Like what?"

As they drove the short drive to her place, she told him about some of her ideas. He looked impressed by the time he pulled into the parking lot.

"You have a talent for organizing things. I'm pretty sure Iian is going to love your ideas. After all, he hired you." He walked around and opened her door.

When she stepped out, she noticed Sara walking by the old antique shop across the way. "Hi." She waved to her.

"Hi." Sara walked over to them. "I was just driving by and saw the "for sale" sign and thought I'd stop and look."

"Are you in the market for an old building?" Luke asked.

She laughed. "Yes actually, I've been thinking about opening a bakery." Sara turned back towards the building. "It's a lot bigger than I'd planned, but I think it'll work." She turned back towards them. "I could even have tables in the front and offer breakfast items. The Golden Oar is great, but they don't open until lunch. I could sell coffee and maybe donuts and muffins."

Luke took Sara's hand in his. "Marry me." He laughed.

"Luke, you know I'd never marry you." She laughed and punched him on the arm. "Do you know if Allison's family still owns the building?"

"I think so, but you might want to ask next time you see her. I expect a party the second that baby arrives. Maybe this time tomorrow?"

"Yeah." Sara bit her lip and turned back towards the building. "Maybe I will ask her. Well," she turned back towards them, "I didn't mean to interrupt your plans. Have a great night." With that she turned and walked back across the street.

"Coffee." Luke and Amber said in unison and laughed all the way up the stairs.

# Chapter Thirteen

Luke watched Amber cook as he sat on her bar stool. She chose to make spinach-stuffed chicken breasts with a side of spaghetti and marinara. It smelled heavenly.

"So, are you disappointed you had to forfeit the game?" she asked as she diced tomatoes.

He laughed. "No, those kids were killing us. It's better to walk away telling ourselves that we could have made a comeback than to know we would have lost big time. Do you know, the last game we played with them, four of us got fouled out, and we didn't have enough team members, so we had to forfeit? We haven't beat them once in the last year. I swear they're getting better, and we are getting worse."

She laughed and he enjoyed the rich sound. He'd been doing a lot of thinking since his gran had passed. He didn't like coming home alone. Sure, now he had Jackie, but it just wasn't the same as having a living, talking person to be with. Especially a woman who smelled sinful and tasted like heaven. He shook his head as he realized she'd asked him a question.

"I'm sorry, my mind was wandering. What did you say?"

She laughed. "I could tell." She took the wooden spoon and stirred the contents in the pan. "I was asking you if Jackie was potty trained yet?"

"Oh, sure. We had that trick down on the first day. Now we're working on shaking. She has sit, lie down, and stay mastered. Shake is not working so well for some reason."

She chuckled, "Well, I wish I could give you pointers, but I've never had any pets." He could hear the sadness in her voice.

"Well, if you want to come over and play with Jackie, you're welcome anytime." He saw her blue eyes light up immediately.

"Really?"

He laughed. "Sure. Besides, it gives me an excuse to see you."

"Yes." She narrowed her eyes and smiled. "Well, there is that."

When they sat down to eat, he enjoyed it so much he had seconds.

"You know, you can always sneak back in the kitchen and be a chef yourself." He smiled as he took the last bite.

"No, I can't stand the heat." She smiled. "Literally." Her phone rang and when she answered it, her face changed. Gone was the happy smile from a second ago.

"Hello, Mother." He watched Amber's body stiffen and saw the light leave her eyes. "No, now's not a good time. I have company." She turned and walked into the hallway. "No, I won't. I'm never going to call Mr. Malone. As far as I'm concerned, Dad can just rot away in his cell. Stop asking me to change my mind. I can't change what I saw that night." He saw her push the button. Getting up, he walked over to her and engulfed her in his arms.

She leaned into him, and he thought she would cry, but instead she shook with anger.

"I don't get how that woman can turn her back on the only child she has, for a man she hasn't been with in years. I mean, she doesn't even know him anymore." She pulled away and looked at his face. "Honestly, the last time I saw him I was ten. I probably wouldn't have recognized him if he walked by me on the street."

He shook his head. What could he say to make it better? "She should believe in you. She should have taken your side. I'm sorry you have to go through that."

She closed her eyes and shook her head. "I got used to it years ago. But she's been pushing for this new appeal. Apparently, they reassess some of the older cases for the holidays. You know, letting convicts that have been rehabilitated out in the holiday spirit and all that. Well, I guess my father would have a pretty strong chance if I'd testify and change my story. After all, the courts took the word of a ten-year-old over that of a full-grown man." She walked away towards the windows, rubbing her forehead. "Not to mention all the evidence they had found."

He walked up behind her and watched the clear night. He was sure that if her lights were off, he'd be able to see all the stars in the sky. Wrapping his arms around her, he pulled her close.

"You're doing the right thing. From what I read— yeah, I snooped and Googled your father." He kissed the back of her head when she chuckled. "Anyway, from what I read, they had a pretty strong case and didn't need your testimony. It was just the icing on the cake."

"Yeah, because of that testimony, I never really had a relationship with my parents. Do you know what's funny?" She turned around towards him, wrapping her arms around his waist. "Shortly after he was put in jail, my father called me and told me how proud he was of me. That was the last time I ever heard from him. I guess he changed his mind after seventeen years in prison."

153

He pulled her face up to his, using just his thumb under her chin. He could see the dull look in her eyes. Seeing the sadness, he realized he'd do anything to see those eyes sparkle again. Leaning down, he took her mouth and lost himself in her taste.

He felt the jolt through her body, then she was pushing him backwards towards her room. The speed in her hands and mouth set his system in overdrive quickly. A zing went through his body, and he knew he had to have her.

Her mouth was pushing him to his limit. He followed her as they shuffled, a disjointed dance, towards the back, to her room. When he reached for the door handle, she pushed him up against the wall and devoured the last thread of his control. He used his mouth as his hands pushed her shirt up and off, then he was running his mouth over her hot body, quickly.

Clothing hit the hallway floor as they punished each other, pushing their limits as they shoved and pulled the clothes off one another. Finally, he stood in the hallway in his boxers as she looked at him in a matching set of blue silk patches that covered the last parts of her, the parts he'd been dying to have. She took a step back, her mouth swollen from his, and walked slowly backwards into her room, wiggling her finger for him to follow. And follow her, he did, until he'd made it halfway across the room.

"Shit." He turned back around and pulled a package from his back pocket. Waving it in the air, he smiled. "Almost forgot."

She smiled and walked over to her night stand. Opening a drawer, she showed him a box inside the top drawer. "Don't worry, I was prepared."

He laughed and grabbed her around the waist and fell with her onto the large bed as their mouths connected again.

She felt like she couldn't get her breath and she was totally fine with it. Luke's hands roamed over her naked skin as she clawed his muscles. She was burning up and needed the speed, needed him to make all the hurt and pain go away. She'd wanted this, wanted him. And now that he was almost fully naked, she realized he was even better looking than she'd first assessed. His chest was only half the appeal; she'd admired his legs throughout the basketball game. She ran her hands over his backside and grabbed hold of his perfect butt. She needed to see it, squeeze it. Running her fingers under the band of his boxers, she started pulling until finally he moved aside so she could pull them away fully.

Moving up to her knees. She pulled them down and tossed them onto her floor. He sat there, half on her bed, half off, smiling at her.

155

"Magnificent." She smiled at him. "How is it that you have the finest butt?"

He laughed. "Basketball. It's all the running."

"Well, I suppose I'll have to start playing."

He shook his head and ran his eyes up and down her. "Lady, you have nothing to worry about." His hands followed the trail his eyes had just taken. She closed her eyes to the enjoyment of him lightly touching her. Her head rolled back, and she lost herself in the feeling. His fingers slowly pulled one bra strap, then the other off her shoulder. He reached behind her and undid the clasp, and watched as the silk fell away.

"Magnificent." He smiled at her as he ran his eyes over her exposed skin.

She'd wanted speed, needed speed, but now, as they sat there, her on her knees, him leaning back on his elbows, she wanted to take her time and enjoy every minute. Leaning closer, she ran her hand up his chest, up his neck, until finally she pulled his face towards her. Just before the kiss, she paused, a breath away. "Are you sure this time?"

She watched his copper eyes heat as he smiled. "Oh, yeah. You?"

"Oh, yeah." She smiled as he pulled her down and took her mouth again. His hands ran over her body, slowly pulling her silk panties down and off her legs, where she kicked them to the floor. His feather light touches set fire to her skin. He ran soft fingers over her newly exposed skin, playing with her folds, torturing her until she squirmed and begged. Then he dipped a finger into her heat, and she almost jumped off the bed, his name on her lips. She was panting, her breath coming in short gasps.

She'd heard it said that sex was always different, depending on the person you were with. Now she knew what they meant. The men she'd been with before paled in comparison to Luke. His touch, his smell, the way he moved, it did something different to her.

He took his time enjoying every inch of her, running his hands and mouth over her skin until she shivered with want. Finally, he moved her until she was lying down next to him. He paused to sheath himself, then smiled as he looked down at her. When he slid into her heat, twin moans sounded as he moved above her. Her legs wrapped around his narrow hips, holding him closer. Her nails dug into his hips as he slowly moved with her. She felt herself building faster than she'd ever built before and begged him for speed.

He smiled down at her then moved faster, using his tongue in her mouth to mimic what he was doing to her down below. And when the lights exploded behind her eyes, he was there to catch her and slowly build her back up. His hands and his mouth seemed to be everywhere as she held onto him again. This time she felt him stiffen and join her for the next explosion.

Amber could feel his heart beating next to hers. She was being crushed and didn't mind. It wasn't that he was heavy, just deadweight. Her hands still gripped his hips, and she realized her hands were cramped. As she slowly moved her fingers she felt him chuckle.

"What?"

"I might just have war scars tomorrow."

"What?"

He leaned up and looked down at her. His hair was a mess from her hands running through it. His eyes were sparkling, causing them to look even more copper in the dull light.

"You know, war scars. From the battle?"

She chuckled and ran her hands smoothly over his hips. When she ran across a few small indents from her nails, she gasped and tried to get a look.

"No, it's okay. Trust me, I didn't feel a thing." He laughed as she looked at the nail marks on his butt and hips.

"Besides, I think I earned them."

She pulled a small round pillow up and covered her face with it. "I've never done that before," she said into the pillow.

"What?" He pulled the pillow away from her face.

"I've never left marks on someone before." She tried to pull the pillow back over her face.

He laughed. "Good." He kissed her again, slowly.

"Listen, I need to head back to the house. I don't want to leave Jackie there all night alone." She saw the worry in his eyes and knew that his concern for the small creature was one of the reasons she felt she was slipping. How could she have let it go this far?

"I'd like to see you on your next day off. Maybe we can head into Edgeview and catch a movie?"

She tilted her head and tried to hold onto him a little longer. "There isn't a movie theater in town."

"There is if you know where to find it." He smiled at her.

"Okay. Now, I'm dying to know more. Sure, but I'm not off until just before Thanksgiving. Especially if Iian is going to be busy with his sister's new baby."

"Oh, yeah! I'd forgotten." He rushed from the bed stark naked to retrieve his pants. When he walked back he had his cell phone in his hands, checking messages.

"Well?" She asked as she pulled on a tank top and shorts.

"Nothing yet. He says she's at the point in the show where she's throwing things at them, though, so he doesn't believe it will be much longer." Luke chuckled.

"Throwing things?" she asked, watching him pull on his pants. He did look mighty fine in blue jeans and nothing else.

"Yeah. Last time, when she gave birth to Lilly, she actually beamed her brother Todd as he brought her a glass of ice." He laughed. "Iian says Conner was an easy birth. He told me Allison was a trooper and didn't even scream. I suppose it has a lot to do with the fact that Lacey is so small." He shook his head. "Anyway, Lacey swears it wasn't that bad. I think everyone else built it up in their minds." He chuckled as he got another text.

"He knows I'm over here. He told me to say "Hi" to you and to let you know he wouldn't be in tomorrow. But he says he knew you'd already know that, so to go back to what we were doing and ignore him."

They laughed. "I guess I should be embarrassed that my boss knows what I'm doing and with whom, but he doesn't really seem like my boss all that much."

"Trust me, he doesn't think he's anyone's boss." Luke walked to the hallway and gathered up the clothes. Dropping them on her chair in the corner, he pulled his shirt from the pile and put it on.

She sighed when his chest was finally covered. Already she was thinking about getting him back in bed. Next time she'd have to make sure to visit him at his place. That way the dog wouldn't be an issue.

"He's been the best boss I've had…well…ever." She smiled, then followed him into her living room.

He sat down and pulled on his shoes.

"When is your next day off?" he glanced up at her.

She walked over to her calendar and looked at her schedule. "Not until next Thursday."

"That's okay, I have a project that I'm about to start. It shouldn't take me more than a week. So, let's say next Thursday it's a date?"

She walked over to where he stood and wrapped her arms around him. "Yes, it's a date." She kissed him and leaned into him as he ran his hands up and down the thin layer of cotton she wore.

Just then his phone beeped with a new message. When he looked down a smile broke out on his face.

"Well, it looks like we have a bouncy baby boy. George Nicholas Stevens weighed in at seven pounds, four ounces and twenty inches long. Apparently he has silver eyes, mom's dark hair, and dad's disposition." He chuckled at that. "Iian says he's a Jordan through and through." Luke looked at her, and she could tell he was proud of his friends. "Everyone is doing fine."

"Oh, how wonderful." She smiled, thinking of seeing the new baby and her new friend. Of course she'd have to work it into her busy schedule over the next few days.

Then he pulled away. "Well, no doubt we'll be seeing each other before Thursday now. I'm sure Iian will do everything he can to have the whole town there to celebrate his new nephew."

# Chapter Fourteen

Two days later, Luke walked into Aaron and Lacey's house with Amber by his side and Jackie in his arms. He knew his friends' house was puppy friendly, and there would be a bunch of kids that could play with Jackie.

Amber had smiled when she'd opened her door and had seen the little puppy in his arms.

"Aaron and Lacey's dogs are going to love playing with Jackie. Besides, it will be good to have her get used to other dogs."

Then he'd gotten a good look at Amber. Her silver dress shined in the lights, and his eyes almost watered with want. He started thinking of a million excuses to give his friends for why they'd be late to the party.

"You look wonderful." He leaned in and kissed her slowly, until Jackie tried to squirm between them and started licking Amber on the chin. Amber laughed and pulled away.

"We could just stay here?" he suggested trying to back her up into her apartment, but she laughed again and pushed him out the door.

"I told you Iian would do everything he could," he said as they walked down the stairs. "Closing the restaurant to celebrate the birth of his nephew is just his style. After all, why have it open, when everyone in town is going to be at the party?"

Little George, as everyone was calling him, was the spitting image of his mom. Knowing how much the Jordan's looked alike, he guessed the little guy was destined to be taller than his mom's five-foot frame. Lacey sat in a large recliner, rocking the little guy and only gave him up when her friends asked to hold him. Aaron stood around with a large grin on his face as he shook everyone's hands.

Amber delivered a present she'd brought for the baby, and since that time she'd been stuck in the room full of women. Luke had been pushed out onto the back deck, where all the men stood talking about sports, hunting, and boating, and spent a good deal of time slapping Aaron on the back.

His mind was never far from Amber, though. His eyes kept wandering back into the house through the large glass doors. He'd even phased out during some of the conversations with his friends.

Aaron and Lacey's dogs ran around the backyard, two grown dogs with Jackie in tow. The three of them played together, chasing balls or sticks that the guys threw their way. It only took fifteen minutes before Jackie was lying at Luke's feet, fast asleep.

When the party was winding down, Luke gathered up Jackie and found Amber in the room full of women, holding a baby. Not George, but someone else's little girl.

"Shh," she said as he sat beside her, Jackie fast asleep in his arms. "Looks like she got tuckered out playing with the big dogs."

"Yeah. Whose little one is this?" He reached over with a finger and gently touched the baby's brown hair. It was feather soft.

"Oh, this is Amber Rose." she smiled. "Great name, huh?"

He smiled. "Yes, Amber's tend to be very strong and yet pretty at the same time." He winked at her.

"She belongs to Lacey's friend from school." She nodded towards the mother sitting across the room holding George. "I get to hold Amber while she holds the new baby. I think it's a pretty sweet deal."

"I agree. She looks a little sturdier than a newborn." He looked over at the small bundle in the woman's arms across the way. He'd held a few newborns in the last couple of years since moving back to Pride. Many of his friends had married and had kids, so naturally he'd been forced to hold the

165

little bundles. Each time his heart would stop, and he'd almost have a panic attack, afraid of dropping or crushing the babies.

"You should see your face." Amber laughed. "No one is going to force you to hold George."

"You don't know this group. Why do you think I'm sitting here with Jackie on my lap? If I'm holding a dog, no one will ask me to hold the baby."

She laughed again. "Are you ready to head out?"

He nodded and ran his finger over the little girl's hair one more time. "You know, when they are this size, they don't look so scary."

She smiled at him. "She's only three months old."

"Really? So they are only scary for three months?"

"No, I would think kids are scary for the rest of your life. Worrying if they are eating the right things, are safe when you're not holding them or they are out of your sight. Then when they grow up, worrying about school, friends, and... Well, you get the picture." He was smiling at her. Not because she was sitting there holding a three-month-old, but because she was sitting there holding a three-month-old and worrying about the full life of any future kids she'd have.

"You really are quite the planner." He laughed when she made a sour face. "Compliment."

"Okay, well, if you hang on just a moment, I'll pass this little one off, and we can head out." He watched her move smoothly, taking the sleeping child with her and gently handing her off to Megan, who was sitting next to Lacey. They said their goodbyes and as they were walking out, they ran into Aaron and Iian playing basketball out front.

"Heading out?" Aaron stopped playing and walked over, scratching Jackie on her head. The dog's eyes rolled, and she started whining.

"Yeah, gotta take my girls home." He liked the sound of it as it rolled off his tongue.

Iian walked over and signed to him that he was just too big of a pussy to play basketball against grown men. Luke just laughed and signed back, "When you see any grown men, call me, and I'll come whoop their butts."

The drive into town was short, but Jackie still managed to fall completely asleep again.

"She likes riding in the car. She hasn't stuck her head out the window yet. She just keeps falling asleep, instead." He watched as Amber rubbed Jackie's head as she lay between them on his truck seat.

She laughed. "Well, it's the purr of the engine. I'm sure when she gets a little older, she'll love to stick her head out the window."

When they drove up to his house, she didn't question him. Instead she picked up Jackie and waited for him to open the door for them.

He didn't know why he felt nervous bringing her back to the house. Maybe because it was the first time he'd ever brought someone here? Maybe because it was her? When he opened the door, Amber set a squirming Jackie down.

"She'll want to go out after the nap." He motioned for her to follow him to the back to the kitchen, where he opened the door and Jackie scrambled out. Amber stood in the doorway of the kitchen, her arms crossed over her chest, looking a little uncomfortable. He walked over to her, and putting his hand on the wall behind her head, leaned in for a kiss. He knew there were several ways to get rid of tension, but this just happened to be his favorite. And he'd been tense since she'd opened her door wearing the silver number.

He tried to keep the kiss light, but she smelled so good and felt even better. Her hands came to his arms, holding him close as he took his time enjoying the taste of her. His hands reached down to her silky legs, pushing them wider, snaking up and pulling her skirt up higher. He moved his hands higher until he'd exposed the silky white lace covering her. Then in one quick move, he pulled the lace aside and slid a finger into her moist heat, causing her to moan and grip onto his arms.

"Luke!" He watched her blue eyes fog as she bit her bottom lip. He couldn't explain it, but just that

168

little nibble made him almost lose control. For a second he could just imagine pulling her up, sheathing himself into her heat, here and now. Fast and hard. Then his eyes met hers, and he knew he needed to slow it down. Instead he played with her heat until her eyes closed, and she leaned back against the wall, holding onto him for support.

Using his leg, he positioned himself so he could hold her up and still enjoy the taste of her neck. With his free hand, he pulled open the top of her dress, exposing the white lace that covered her there. He dipped his head and used his mouth to wet the lace until her nipples puckered through the light material. Then he pulled it aside and touched his tongue to her heated skin. Her hands flew to his hair, holding him to her as his other hand continued to plunder below. She arched and moaned, trying to pull him closer, demanding more. But he held back, just using his hands and mouth to please her and build her up.

"Luke, please." She pulled on his shirt, trying to get the buttons undone. He chuckled and leaned back, grabbing her hands in one of his and holding them over her head.

"No, let me take my time. I want to savor every inch." He ran his free hand down the front of her dress, opening the small buttons down the front, exposing her all the way. Finally, she stood with her dress wide open, covered only by a white silk bra, panties, and her thin silver heels. Her hands were again clasped in his, held above her head, pushing her perfect breasts together.

She took his breath away. Her dark hair fell down over her shoulders, and her blue eyes were cloudy with desire. He could see her pulse at every sensitive spot on her body. He used his free hand to run up and down her soft skin. He knew he couldn't wait much longer, but he needed this one last touch.

What was he doing to her? He was still fully dressed and the feel of his clothes next to her naked skin only heated her. Her legs were spread wide, her arms held tightly over her head, and all she could think about was having him inside her. She felt like she was the main course, held there for him to see and use as he pleased, totally exposed, but loving every second of it.

Then his hand ran over her, and she lost the ability to breathe. He cupped her face, running his fingers down her neck, across her lace bra, over her peaked nipples, stopping for just a quick circle around each one, then continuing down a path that took him past her belly button and over her hips, until finally he reached where she wanted him. His hand loosened on her wrists above her head, and he leaned down in front of her and set his tongue to the same spot. Her hands went into his dark hair, holding him still as he lapped her up.

His hands went to her thighs, gently nudging them wider. Her back arched off the wall as his fingers joined his mouth, torturing her, causing her to moan. She'd never wanted someone as badly as she wanted Luke now. She could feel herself building and thought she'd lose it if he didn't take her now. Then he pulled away and stood up. He turned her until she placed her hands on the wall. Holding her two feet away from the wall, he moved her dress aside, finally pulling it off her shoulders so now she truly was just wearing a bra and panties and heels in his kitchen. He ran his hands down her shoulders and her back, then bent her over slightly, using his thighs to spread her legs again. She took a few deep breaths, knowing what was coming, silently begging him to hurry. She heard him unzip his pants and open a condom package, and she wished he would go faster. She was burning and she needed him. The anticipation was killing her. She arched her hips when he touched her there. Holding onto her, he slowly slid into her as she closed her eyes and moaned with relief. He adjusted his feet and took a better hold of her hips, then started moving faster. He moved her hair gently to one side, then leaned in and placed a kiss on her exposed neck and ear.

"Do you like this?" he whispered into her ear.

"Mmm, God, yes. Please, Luke."

His hand ran up the front of her, cupping her and pinching her nipples slightly. "You feel so good, Amber. I want to feel you tighten up around me as you come." He started moving faster until she leaned her head back against him and cried out his name.

"Good. Now…" He turned her, pushing her back against the wall. He took her left thigh, and holding it up high, entered her again in a quick thrust. "Again." He took her mouth in a deep kiss that sent the fires jumping in every nerve ending throughout her entire body.

His shoulders held them against the wall as he reached down and took her right thigh in his other hand, pulling it up until she wrapped her legs around his hips. He thrust faster and deeper.

Finally, when she knew she couldn't hold on any longer, he kissed her and tensed as she joined him.

Minutes later, Amber heard whining. It took her a minute to figure out what it was. Her legs were still wrapped around his waist, his shoulders still holding them against the wall. She opened her eyes and saw the darkened kitchen. The sun had set while her eyes had been closed. Then she heard the scratching and whining again.

"Luke, Jackie wants in." He shook his shoulders, smiling.

"Hmm? Oh." He released her legs. She moved and stood back up on shaky legs. "I'm sorry." He waited until she looked steady, then bent down to retrieve her dress.

"You're sorry?" She smiled at him and took her dress.

"Yeah, um. I should have waited and taken you upstairs."

She laughed. "You don't have to be sorry. I had planned on taking you on the kitchen table if you hadn't intervened." She watched him walk over to the back door and open it for Jackie. The little dog quickly bolted in the door, sniffed his feet, and then ran into the laundry room.

"She wants her dinner." He walked towards the laundry room. "Um, you don't plan on going anywhere do you?" He looked at her, pleading.

"Where would I go?" She smiled as she finished buttoning up her dress.

"Good, um, if you're hungry…"

"No." She smiled. "Luke, feed the dog, then take me upstairs."

His smile was quick, and she laughed as he rushed into the laundry room to feed Jackie.

# Chapter Fifteen

When Amber opened her eyes the next morning, she was looking directly into a large alien's face. She would have screamed, but she knew that face all too well. It was the alien from the game Chris had been addicted to. Modark, the alien, had been fighting against evil on his home planet of...She squinted her eyes, trying to remember the planet's name. Oh, well, she thought, it'll come to me. Anyway, the chances that Luke would have a full-size standup cardboard cutout of the character she partially blamed for the failure of her past relationships was almost laughable. Especially since she was lying naked in Luke's room, which was stocked full of images of Modark and Korkin, the villain.

Looking around, she saw images of the planets, battle ships, weapons, and more characters from the game. How had she ended up here? Oh, yeah! By having some of the best sex she'd ever had. She closed her eyes and tried not to moan. Luke was lying next to her, his arm slung over her hips. She could feel his breath on her shoulder.

She thought about trying to sneak out of the bed, but then he moved, and she knew he was awake.

"Luke, I've got to get going. I work in three hours." He looked at her and smiled.

"Three hours is a long time from now." He tried to pull her closer.

"Yes, it is, but I hear Jackie begging to be let out." That got his attention.

"Oh, poor baby. I usually let her out sooner." He jolted from the bed, slid on a pair of jeans that looked like they'd seen better days, then bolted from the room, only to stick his head back in and say, "Don't go anywhere." Then he was gone again.

Where did he think she'd disappear to? Looking around the room, she walked over and grabbed one of his t-shirts and put it on. It hit her mid-thigh, and she felt sufficiently covered. She looked around his room. He really was a man-boy. There were more toys in here than most ten-year-olds had. The one difference was that they were all from the one game, Alien Engagement. She knew he'd told her it was his job, not something he did for fun, but really, how could he not think of this as fun? Even the mouse pad for his computer had an image of Modark. Leaning over, she looked more closely at it. Modark, prince of planet Odge. She snapped her fingers. That was the name, Odge.

She spent another two minutes looking around before deciding to shower. His bathroom was huge and from the looks of it, recently remodeled. The tan tiles and updated look of the bathroom seemed in total contrast to the rest of the house. When she turned on the large shower, she was jolted to realize that there were multiple shower heads spraying her from all directions. She'd planned on dodging the cold spray until it had warmed up, but now, cold water hit her from every angle. She must have squealed, because Luke came running in. He took one look at her through the clear shower doors and started laughing.

"Got hit with the cold, huh?" He walked towards her, slowly removing his jeans.

"There should be a warning on this thing." She pushed her wet hair out of her face. "I didn't even see the other shower heads." She looked around, holding up her hands to block some of the water from hitting her in the face.

"Here." He stepped into the shower just as the water turned warm. Then he twisted the handle to the left and some of the shower heads turned off. "Turn it this way if you just want the main one there." He pointed to the large one overhead. To get the full deal, twist it—"

"No!" She grabbed his arm. "I get it."

He laughed and pulled her close. "Looks like we'll save a little time by showering together."

She wrapped her arms around his shoulders to steady herself. "I'm all for conserving water," she said, then she reached up and kissed him.

An hour later, as he drove her back to her place, she asked, "So, what are you doing Thursday?"

"Thursday?" He looked over at her.

"Thanksgiving." She watched his eyes dull.

"Thursday is Thanksgiving?" Even though he was looking straight ahead, she could see the sadness enter his face.

"Luke?" She reached out and touched his arm.

"I'd totally forgotten. Gran would have had me put out all the decorations. I forgot to put them out."

"It's okay." She squeezed his arm lightly.

"No, it's not. I didn't even know it was Thanksgiving. I guess I've been so busy with everything else, I'd forgotten about it."

"Well, there's still time." She smiled as he looked over at her.

"Yeah, I guess you're right." He smiled and looked back at the road.

"You can even have people over if you want," she said as he pulled into the parking lot of her place.

"Yeah, I suppose I could. I've never hosted a party before."

"I could help you. Hosting parties is kind of my specialty."

"Well, I suppose so. It's kind of short notice, but why not?"

"Good, it's settled. You invite everyone, and I'll take care of everything else." She leaned over and kissed him quickly, then jumped from the truck. She was so excited about the possibility of planning out his party that she didn't even care that Patty and a few of the other women smiled as she got out of Luke's truck wearing the same dress she'd worn to yesterday's party. Instead, she waved and smiled, then rushed up the stairs to get ready for work.

By the time she made it to the restaurant, she had a full list of things that she'd need going in her head. She sailed through work the next few days. Maybe it was the excitement of working on a project, or the fact that she'd finally gotten to talk to Iian about some of her changes. Luke had been right; Iian had not only liked them all, but given her the go-ahead to start making them.

The major change was making the back room more "kid friendly" for birthday parties. She'd noticed the need early on. Most parents brought family and friends here for birthdays or anniversaries. There were almost always small kids involved, and they would spend their time running around looking bored.

She'd given Iian a few ideas to help the cause, and Iian had taken her hint and ordered the room to

178

be repainted and decorated. The workers would start shortly after Thanksgiving and finish just before Christmas.

When they were done, Amber imagined the room would be perfect for showers, birthdays, anniversaries, and even graduation parties, without taking away from the main dining experience.

She'd also pitched her idea of building a large fish tank wall to separate the bar area and the main dining hall. That way, bar goers, who tended to be loud, wouldn't disturb the family dining a few feet away.

"We can put exotic fish in it so people have something to look at while waiting for a table or just eating or drinking."

"I like it, but I'm not sure how it would work." Conversations with Iian tended to be slow, so she'd come prepared. Pulling out her sketch pad, she showed him a few drawings she'd made. One showed the floor plans with a large V where the tank would be. Then she pulled out another drawing that showed how the wall would look. It was a custom tank that would sit three feet off the ground and be two feet wide. She'd worked with a company in Portland that made custom tanks, and she handed Iian their business card. "They could give you an estimate on the costs. I think you will see an increase in sales at the bar, because the bar will be separated from the dining area, and people won't feel like they are on display. I've noticed your bar sales aren't as high as they could be because of this."

Iian liked the idea so much he got on the company's website, and they spent the next hour looking over the information. She called them and relayed all the details. They had an opening the week after Thanksgiving to drive down and take a look to give them a better estimate.

She left work and headed home. She'd made plans to stay at Luke's house tonight and was running a little late heading over there, but she had a few boxes of items at her place for the party. She had the next two days off, and the party was tomorrow. She was excited for it, but she was just as excited to get back to work on Monday to start organizing the changes that would happen over the next few weeks.

She parked and started walking up her stairs and was halfway up before she saw the woman standing on her landing. At first Amber thought it was another woman from town dropping off baked goods, or another well-wisher. But then the woman spoke, and Amber felt a bolt of lightning go down her spine.

"Hello, Amber," her mother said, looking down at her from the top of the stairs.

Amber's hand fell away from the railing. She knew her chin had dropped, and she probably looked like a dead fish staring up at her mother. It had been eight years since she'd seen the woman last. In that time, her mother had aged and grown very frail. She wore thick glasses and her hair was longer and tied in a tight bun at the nape of her neck. Her long skirt flowed all the way to her shoes. The neckline of her shirt covered every inch of her underneath a large coat. Amber noticed the long sleeves went past her wrists. She looked like a woman who had stepped out of the past. Almost every inch of her was covered with material.

It took her almost a full minute to recover. "Hello, Mother." Amber finished walking up the stairs and opened her door. The chill in the air forced her to invite her mother inside.

After removing her coat and hanging it up on the rack, she turned to her mother. "Can I take your coat?"

"No, that won't be necessary. I won't be here long. I've come to ask you face-to-face to reconsider going to the court tomorrow for the special holiday hearing. Your father needs you. This is our last chance to fix the injustices served him all those years ago."

Amber's headache instantly came on. Her eyes narrowed, and she could see a gray film cover her vision. She rubbed her forehead. "I've told you what happened that night. I wasn't lying. I saw it with my own two eyes."

"The eyes of a nine-year-old. You always had such an imagination. If you'd just go with me, explain that you question what you saw. That there

181

is a chance that you didn't actually see it that way—
"

"Mother, stop!" Amber rubbed her head and walked to the windows, not really seeing the new snow as it started to fall. "I'm not doing this anymore. If you won't stand behind me, then you can stand on your own. I won't go to the hearing tomorrow. I won't ever tell someone I didn't witness my father killing a man in cold blood. I won't lie. If you can't accept that then I'd preferred never to hear from you again." She kept her back to the room, not wanting her mother to see the tears streaming down her face. Her back was stiff, and when she heard her front door open and close, she knew she'd gotten her answer.

She'd been standing there looking out the window for an hour when she heard the door open behind her. Spinning around, she saw Luke standing there covered in snow, a worried look on his face.

"Are you okay? I've been calling you for the last forty minutes." He shook the snow from his coat and hung it on the rack, then walked towards her. She hadn't realized she was standing in a dark room until he flipped on the lights. When he saw her face, he rushed over to her and engulfed her in a hug.

"What's wrong?" He kissed her head.

"I'm sorry. I forgot my cell phone in the Jeep. I was just running in to grab those boxes, but she was there on my landing."

"Who?" He pulled back and looked at her.

"My mother. She came to try to convince me to go to my father's hearing tomorrow." She leaned against his chest and closed her eyes, realizing that her eyes stung.

"I'm sorry," he whispered. "Are you okay?"

She shook her head no. "But I will be. I told her that if she wouldn't take my side, then I didn't want to hear from her again. She left without another word." It stung. Stung so much that fresh tears streamed down her face.

He pulled her face up and looked her in the eyes, gently wiping the tears from her cheeks. Then he bent down and kissed her lips. "I'm so sorry, Amber. I can't begin to understand what you're going through, other than the feeling of loss."

She took a deep breath, and looking into his copper eyes, realized he'd been through much worse lately. Now, this party meant everything to him and to her. It was a way to tell themselves that this was their family. The people they'd invited tomorrow had replaced the blood relatives they'd lost, and the ones that had simply chosen not to be there.

She took a deep breath again and smiled up at him. "We have a party to plan, and I'm running late getting everything over to your house." She pulled back and wiped her eyes. "Now, if you'll help me carry down these boxes, we can get going."

When she opened the door to help him out, she gasped, "Oh! It's snowing." He laughed behind her.

"You stood there looking out a large window for an hour and just now noticed it was snowing?"

"Well, I was preoccupied." She laughed. "Okay, it does sound a little weird. I supposed I was reliving that night over and over again, trying to determine if I'd really seen what I'd thought I'd seen." She opened the back of her Jeep so he could put the box inside and get it out of the snow. She closed it and turned to look at him. The snow hit his hair and instantly melted, making his hair look darker. Large flakes landed on his eyelashes and cheeks. "You forgot your hat and gloves." She smiled at him.

"I know. I seem to be forgetting a lot now that my grandmother isn't around to remind me all the time." He pulled her into a hug and kissed her as the snow silently fell around them.

# Chapter Sixteen

By the time the first guest arrived the next day, Luke's house shined like it hadn't in years. He and Amber had spent several hours cleaning and reorganizing. She'd helped him optimize the space so that the room flowed better—her words, not his. He had to admit, it did open the place up a lot. Now he didn't feel like he was going to be constantly hitting his shins on the chair as he walked by.

She'd even helped him clean and organize his food shelves. She told him with this system—yeah, she'd called it a system—he'd be more efficient in the kitchen. He replied, "The last time we were in this kitchen together, I didn't hear you complaining about my efficiency." He'd followed it up with a loud smack of a kiss and a quick slap on her butt.

He should have known that Allison, Iian, and Conner would be the first ones to show up. Conner was a sturdy-looking toddler, and he played with Jackie in the kitchen while Iian helped with the finishing touches in the kitchen.

"Not that I don't trust your cooking. After all, I did spend a summer teaching you everything you know," Iian had signed to him.

"Right, then I taught you everything you know about women. That's why you're married to hot Ally." They laughed as they worked in the kitchen. He was just putting the sweet potatoes in the oven when Todd and Megan walked in.

"Come to give us a hand?"

"God, no. Don't you know by now not to trust my wife in the kitchen?" Todd laughed and kissed his wife. She smiled and set her youngest, Riley, down on the floor to play with the puppy. Her fly-away blond hair had a pretty red bow in it today.

"Where are your other two rug rats?" He asked Megan as he kissed her cheek.

"Oh, they're coming. They are just seeing the new baby. Aaron and Lacey showed up right behind us." As if on cue, two kids came running into the room. Matthew, a rambunctious eight-year-old, came first, and his sister, Sara, wasn't far behind him. They both plopped down on the ground and started playing with Jackie.

"Kids, say hello to everyone first." Megan sat down at the kitchen table.

"Hello," both kids said without looking up from the dog. Everyone laughed.

By the time all his guests had arrived, the place was packed and smelled of wonderful food. The kitchen table was loaded with dishes people had brought. Folding chairs and tables were brought in from the garage. Everyone made their way through the kitchen, grabbing heaping plates of food, then they filled every chair in his house to sit down and eat.

He enjoyed the feeling of having friends over and knew it wouldn't be the last party he'd throw. He sat next to Amber as they ate at the main table in the dining room, surrounded by their only family, and he knew the path he wanted to take. He wanted Amber to be sitting beside him for the next party, and the next, and the next. His heart skipped a beat when he thought of her not being there. He could only imagine that this was how his grandparents had felt about one another.

He'd only know her for two months, yet she was everything he wanted for his future. Now he just needed to figure out how to tell her and show her he was the right one for her.

After the paper plates had been disposed of, and the dishes had been handled, everyone sat around and listened to Todd and Patty play the violin and piano in the front room. Luke knew that Iian could play piano as well, but he hadn't attempted it in years, since losing his hearing.

Amber sat next to Luke on the couch holding George.

"Such an old fashion name for such a little guy." Amber gently rubbed George's dark hair.

"It was Todd, Lacey, and Iian's father's name. He died in the same accident that took Iian's hearing."

Amber looked at Luke.

It was Iian's eighteenth birthday and his father had taken him out sailing, something they'd always done. Apparently there was a bad storm. They found Iian later, and he was pretty banged up and had lost his hearing. Iian can only remember bits and pieces. He thinks his father threw him on the lifeboat just before getting hit by lightning. He swears his father saved his life."

"Oh, how sad." Amber looked down at the tiny baby. "Well, from the sounds of it, you're named after a really great man." She kissed the baby's nose, and another piece of the puzzle he'd been missing was found.

It was wonderful spending the weekend at Luke's place. The party had been a huge success. She really was starting to feel like part of the town. Everyone was so friendly that she doubted she'd ever want to leave. She was trying to focus on the good and not on the visit from her mother. She was due back at work on Monday morning to meet with the contractors, but for the weekend, she pretended she had a different life. She imagined this was her life, living in a huge Victorian house on a country road in a small town along the Oregon coast, with her dog and her man.

The only reminder of what might be coming was the constant view of game items in his bedroom. When she tried to bring it up, he laughed.

"If you don't like the stuff, I can move it into my gran's sewing room down the hall. I've been thinking of turning that into an office anyway." It seemed to her that instead of winning the battle, she'd only postponed it, but she didn't mention it the rest of the weekend. Instead, she spent her time laughing and enjoying every moment with Luke and Jackie. The snow hadn't stuck so the backyard was a mud pile. Every time Jackie went out, they had to use a towel to dry her off. Amber had gotten it in her head to give the girl a bath, which had just soaked them and made them both smell like wet dog.

She did enjoy the hour-long, hot shower they'd taken together afterwards, though.

By Sunday night, she was feeling a little sad that she had to head back to her place.

"Why don't you stay one more night? You can leave first thing in the morning." He made a sad face, puckering his bottom lip out.

"I wish I could. But I have laundry to do tonight and I really do need a full night's rest. We both know that I'd never get that if I stay here."

He smiled. "I didn't hear you complaining last night." He pulled her closer. Her coat was already on, and she had been trying to get her gloves on. She pushed him away playfully.

"No. No complaints from me. But I do need to go." She kissed him again and picked up her overnight bag.

"Well, fine. Give me a call when you get home. You know, so I know you got there okay."

She smiled. "Okay." She leaned in and kissed him again. "Goodnight."

She drove home in silence, and when she turned onto Main Street she was stunned to see that the Christmas lights were already hanging across the street, and on every light post hung large wreathes with red bows. She really did like this town.

It took her a few minutes to get situated. She had laundry going before she called Luke. When he answered, he sounded out of breath.

"Is everything okay?"

"Yeah, yeah. Well..." He took a deep breath and she could hear him moving around. "Actually, right after you left, Jackie decided to start acting up. She dragged my good jeans—you know; the ones I always wear—all the way downstairs." She knew the ones and couldn't really call them his good ones.

"The faded blue jeans with the holes in the knees?"

"Yeah, those are the ones. Anyway, she dragged them all the way downstairs, then got out the back door with them and drug them through the mud. They're ruined. Totally ruined." He actually sounded hurt, and she laughed and laughed until her sides hurt.

When she finally stopped, the other side of the call was quiet. "Luke?"

"Yeah?" He still sounded hurt.

"You can always buy new jeans."

"Do you know how long it took me to break those in?"

"Twenty years?" She laughed some more, and this time he joined her.

"Okay, so it's not so bad. I just don't know how she did it all so quickly. She was such a good girl when you were here." He left the statement hanging.

"Is that supposed to be some sort of guilt trip?" She smiled and snuggled under her blanket on the couch. The heater was just kicking in, warming the place.

"Did it work?" She laughed again. "What are you wearing?" His voice changed and got deeper, more like a whisper.

She smiled. "Are you trying to have phone sex with me?"

"Is it working?" She laughed again.

"Well, maybe. What are *you* wearing?" she asked in a breathless voice.

"Not my favorite blue jeans." They both laughed.

The next morning, she felt like she still hadn't gotten enough sleep, probably due to spending half the night talking to Luke on the phone. He kept trying to tell her how late it was, but she just didn't want to get off the line with him. It was her own fault. She walked into the restaurant at eight the next morning wishing for a strong cup of coffee. Good thing she worked at a restaurant. Less than fifteen minutes later, armed with a large cup, she opened the doors for the construction crew and showed them what was being done.

Several hours later, just before the lunch rush, the men from the fish tank company showed up. Iian had arrived shortly after her that morning, and they'd spent a good deal of their time taking measurements and discussing what they wanted.

"My brother drew this up." He handed her a piece of paper.

On the sketch, instead of a large V, there was a somewhat oval-shaped semi-circle. The smooth lines would enhance the shape of the current bar. She could just imagine the fun shape and how it would look from both sides.

"Wonderful. I like it so much better."

They spent some time walking over the carpeted area, trying to find the right spot. When the two men from the fish tank company showed up, she told them exactly what they wanted.

The estimate they provided was lower than she'd imagined, especially since they had added a custom-shaped curved tank instead of two square ones.

"We can still keep two tanks if you want. One for fresh fish, the other for salt water. We'd use a divider here," said the company's owner, Mark, pointing to the middle of Todd's drawing. "We'd use extra thick material here. Add another filter and pump below."

"Wonderful. Now all we'll need is some fish." She smiled.

"We can get those for you, too. What kind do you want?" She translated to Iian, who pulled out a list and smiled.

She was happy that he'd come prepared and was excited about her idea.

When she walked into the empty back room at the end of her shift, the workers had made enormous progress. They'd used the back doors to haul all the old carpet and ceiling tiles out. For the most part, the place had been gutted in one day. She knew firsthand that it sometimes took longer to put something back together than it did to take something apart.

When she arrived at home, she wasn't surprised to see Luke sitting in his truck. There was a small Christmas tree in the back of his truck, and when she walked by, he jumped out with a large bag.

"I've got something for you." He smiled.

"I can see." She looked at the tree.

"I figured you'd have one of those plastic ones. There's just no replacement for the real deal." He smiled and handed her the bag. "You carry that, I'll carry this." He pulled the medium-sized tree from the back of his truck.

She rushed ahead of him and unlocked the door. Then she set the bag down on the table and held the door open as Luke maneuvered the tree inside.

"I think it should go by the window, just in the corner there," she said as he walked towards the windows. "Oh, I have a stand. Hang on." She rushed from the room and came back with a small green and red stand.

They took a few minutes to set it up. He lay on the floor while she held the tree, making sure it was completely vertical.

"There." He dusted his hands and stood back, next to her. "Now all we need are lights and ornaments."

"It's a good thing I have some of those." She smiled and went back to her office, then came out with a large box. "Actually, I have lots of ornaments. I'll get the other box."

They spent the next hour stringing up the tree, hanging each ornament where she wanted it. He laughed at her when she moved several around to 'fill holes' as she called it. Then she made hot chocolate, and they sat in the dark, watching the chasing lights reflect off the glass.

"All you need is a fireplace and some Christmas music," he said as she snuggled next to him.

"Don't forget the presents for under the tree."

"Oh, presents." He stood up and flipped on the kitchen light. "Where did you put it?"

"Put what?" She watched him from across the room.

"The bag with the box in it."

"Oh, there." She pointed to the table by the door.

He walked over and grabbed the bag, then moved back over and sat next to her.

"My gran left this for you." He pulled out an old box. "I found it this morning in her room. There was a note for me. There's one for you, too." He handed her a note.

She took it with shaky hands. "Why would she leave me something?"

"I don't know. My note said for me not to open it, but to bring it to you, instead. I didn't want her holding a grudge on me in heaven, so I obeyed her."

He handed her the box. She held it on her lap and slowly opened the note.

*Amber, I know we only met once, but I saw how Luke's eyes lit up around you and could tell you were the one I needed to pass this precious information to. I can't trust the boy with a pan of brownies, so there is no way I'm giving him the recipe for them. Guard it and remember, chocolate cures all. -- Margaret Kennedy.*

Amber laughed and opened the box slowly. Inside was a treasure trove of recipes of every kind: chicken dumpling, turkey pot pie, cakes, breads. There were even recipes for ketchup and mayonnaise. "Who makes their own mayonnaise?" Amber asked Luke, who was looking over her shoulder.

"There isn't a recipe for brownies in there?" Luke was straining to see over her shoulder.

She pulled the box aside and quickly shut the lid. "No, you don't. This is for me, not you." She smiled and walked into her kitchen, setting the box on the top shelf. When she turned around, he was right behind her. He moved her until her back hit the refrigerator. His hands went to her hips, hers to his shoulders.

"My gran must have liked you a lot to trust you with her treasures." He placed a kiss on her lips.

"Hmm. She knew a good cook when she saw one." He laughed.

"I think she just trusted you more with her brownie recipe. She would never bake them while I watched. When I was at MIT I tried to make them, but I could never get the recipe right."

"You actually went to MIT?" She pulled back and looked at him.

"Yeah, for a few years. Until my grandfather passed. Then I came back here to be closer to my grandmother. She needed me." He leaned in and kissed her neck.

"Luke, I've been at work all day. I smell like food and sawdust."

He pulled back. "Sawdust?"

"Oh, yeah, I forgot to tell you over the weekend with everything that was going on. Iian and I are rebuilding the Golden Oar. Well, not rebuilding it completely." She smiled.

Luke was so interested in hearing her story and seeing the changes to the place, he promised to drop by for lunch tomorrow so she could show him everything they had planned.

"You know; I've been thinking of changing a few things around the house myself. When I moved back home, I redid the bathroom. Gran's shower was about two feet too short for me, and she insisted that I fix it to make it more comfortable. The rest of the place could use a fresh...well... everything." He laughed. "It is kind of decorated in mid-eighties." He looked at her. "Maybe you can come over on your night off and give me some of your thoughts." He smiled and pulled her close.

"Luke, if you want me to spend the night, all you have to do is ask." She kissed his lips.

"I want you to spend the night. All of your free nights." He leaned his head against hers. "I've been lonely without you. The place feels empty. Jackie feels it, too. Why do you think she acts up when you aren't around?"

Amber felt herself starting to shake. "Luke, I don't mind spending a few nights here and there. But I have my own place. I tried living with my last boyfriend. It didn't end very well."

He pulled back like he'd been slapped. "I'm not your ex."

"I'm not saying you are. I'm just not ready for that kind of commitment."

"I know." He walked to the window next to the tree, then turned back to her. "It's snowing again. I'd

198

better get going." He walked to the door. Her heart felt heavy. She knew she had trust issues, but she was sure she'd handled the situation well. After all, they'd only know each other for two months.

"Goodnight." She held the door open as he walked by. "Luke?" She stopped him. "I just need some more time."

He looked at her like he was still hurt. "I know. I'm sorry. I didn't mean to pressure you. I hope you'll still come over and help me plan out my changes. You did such a great job moving everything around so it works better. I think you'd be great at helping me decide what to do with the place." He ran his hand down the side of her face gently. "Goodnight, Amber." He leaned in and placed a soft kiss on her nose.

After he left, she stood by the Christmas tree with its flashing lights and watched the snow fall.

# Chapter Seventeen

Luke drove into the Golden Oar's parking lot the next day feeling very confident that he knew what he wanted. But when he walked in and saw Amber, his confidence faltered. She was standing near the back room wearing the black pants and red top that were the new uniforms for the restaurant. They looked very appealing on her. It amazed him how beautiful she was. She looked up and waved at him as he started walking towards her.

She handed the man she'd been talking to a piece of paper and he walked away. "Luke, you made it." She looked a little relieved, like she hadn't been sure if he'd come today or not.

"I wouldn't miss it. I'm dying to find out what you've got planned." He looked around. "Is the large sheet of plastic to keep the dust down?"

"That and the noise. I've put up a "pardon our dust" sign, but for the most part, I think we've had more people in here since we started remodeling. I think they're curious. I think they're more curious about all the mess than enjoying all our Christmas decorations." She motioned to all the wreaths and ornaments around the place. Then she took his hand and walked him around the plastic sheet. "You can't really tell anything yet, since they are still in the breakdown stage. But this is what we have planned. Todd stopped by yesterday and helped me sketch these out. Isn't he great?" She showed him a folder that had been sitting on a desk.

The sketches showed exactly what she'd described to him. He could imagine the large back room turning into a more open area with a stage and a dance floor.

"In the corner, Iian is going to put a couple of video games." She laughed. "I never would have thought of it. He said something about Pac-Man and was off hunting on his computer to get the games."

Luke laughed. "I'll bet." He thought of stopping by and talking to Iian about another game idea. "This all looks wonderful. You say they are going to have it done before Christmas?"

"Oh, yes. There are no real structural changes. Just paint, flooring and ceiling tiles. The stage is movable so if a party doesn't need it, it will fold up."

"You said something about a fish tank?"

"Here." She smiled and grabbed his hand again, pulling him past the wall of plastic towards the bar.

"It's going to sit here." She handed him another drawing. Again, he could just imagine the separation that would give both large areas more privacy.

"You really have a talent for this kind of stuff. I hope everything's done for the Christmas party the Jordan's always throw."

"Oh." She bit her bottom lip. "Christmas party?"

"Yes, don't get any ideas. This one's all Lacey's doing. She enjoys pulling out all the stops for this one party."

"Oh." She looked a little hurt.

"Don't worry. There are plenty of other parties you can plan. My birthday is coming up in February." He smiled.

She smiled back at him. "Did you want some lunch?"

"No, I ate. I'm just heading over to play."

"Oh, right, it's game day. I wish I could be there for the Hornets and Sasquatch's rematch."

"That's okay, maybe next time." He placed a quick kiss on her lips.

He made a quick stop to Iian's office and then they left together to head out to the game. When he made it back home, he was sorer than he'd been in years. Every inch of him ached. How could a bunch of teens whoop their butts so bad?

There were a few messages on his computer, and he ended up staying up all night to fix a few bugs in his latest product. Launch day was scheduled for Friday, and he was just as excited as he'd been the first time a product of his hit the open market.

Now all he needed was someone to share that excitement with. He looked around. Jackie was curled up on his bed, a spot she'd taken to since Amber had vacated the spot. Looking over at his clock, he realized it was almost noon the next day. If he got a few hours' sleep, he could probably make it over to Amber's place when she got off work. He crawled into bed with Jackie and smiled when the small dog got up off her pillow and came over to snuggle against his chest.

It was hard to explain the love he felt when she leaned her little head up and licked his chin. Her sad eyes looked at him and he smiled. Another moment that he wished he had someone to share with.

He woke several times to let Jackie out and give her food, but he kept crawling back into bed. His eyes were heavy. Maybe he was coming down with the flu? He didn't feel like he had a fever, he was just really tired.

The last time he looked at the clock it was one in the morning, and he thought he could sleep for another eight hours straight.

When he did wake, it was still dark. He was confused and looked at his clock. Seven. He didn't know if it was seven in the morning or at night. He grabbed his phone and realized it was seven at night. He'd slept a whole day away, eighteen hours straight, and he felt like he hadn't moved a muscle that entire time.

He moved to the end of the bed and felt every muscle in his body revolt. His head was dull, like he'd just drunk a tub of tequila. His shirt and shorts were a little sweaty. There was no doubt he had a fever now. When he stood, he felt weak and had to grab onto the night stand.

He hated being sick. Jackie sat on the floor, looking at him like she was in trouble.

"Sorry, baby. I know I didn't let you out. If you made a mess in the house, don't worry about it. I'll clean it up later." She turned in circles and followed him into the bathroom.

After a very hot shower and a few aspirin, he downed a dozen ounces of orange juice from the fridge. He cleaned up a puddle by the back door as he let Jackie out.

He started feeling better and decided he felt good enough to head over and see if Amber was off work tonight.

The holiday season was in full swing in Pride. Amber had never truly understood what Christmas meant until she'd ended up here. Everywhere she looked decorations and lights hung. The storefront at O'Neil's was transformed into a wonderland filled with nativity scenery, and a large Christmas tree stood in the window.

It seemed everywhere Amber went, people would stop and chat with her about her holiday plans. She'd been invited to countless dinners, parties, and plays. But the biggest and best party everyone was talking about was the Christmas party at the Golden Oar. It seemed Lacey knew how to throw a party.

"You see, dear, it all started a few years back, before Lacey and Aaron were married. They threw a joint party at his house for New Year's. Well, the next year, they moved it forward to Christmas and had it at the restaurant. It was such a success, they continued the tradition. Now it's just assumed that everyone will be there." Patty finished bagging her items. She smiled at the dog ball Amber had picked up for Jackie. "How is that cutie doing? I bet she's being spoiled rotten."

"Jackie? Yes, I haven't seen her in a few days, but I hear she's causing quite the mess lately. I hear that along with new jeans, Luke now needs a new pair of tennis shoes." Amber tried not to laugh.

"Well, that's what puppies do." Patty smiled. "So, will you two be heading to the party together?"

Amber had been wondering the same thing. Luke hadn't talked to her about the party. Actually, in the last two days since she'd seen him at the restaurant, she hadn't talked to him at all.

Maybe he was still hurt about the other night. He hadn't acted like it the other day, but then again, she hadn't given him much time to talk either. She'd just walked around, chatting about the changes being made at the restaurant.

By the time she walked back into her apartment, she'd talked herself into quite a state. She began questioning if he ever wanted to see her again. Maybe this was his way of pulling away? After all, she'd pretty much compared him to Chris, her ex-boyfriend. She'd never really given him a chance to explain what he did for a living. All she knew is that it had something to do with video and computer games.

She just couldn't imagine a full-grown man making a living working on games. It wasn't as if she didn't like games. When she'd been dating Chris, she'd played Alien Engagement with him on several occasions. The game was very addictive, but she'd known when to shut it down. Chris hadn't. She guessed that was her question about Luke. Did he know when to shut down playing and come back into real life? She knew his past, that he'd given up school—at MIT, no less—to come back and take care of his grandmother. Chris wouldn't have gotten off the couch cushion to visit his mother, let alone move across the country to take care of her.

Luke had wanted her to move in with him, at least that's what she thought he'd been hinting at.

Letting Chris move in with her had been the largest mistake she'd ever made. Their relationship had been fun up until that point, just like her relationship with Luke. Sure, there was the weekend she'd spent nights at Luke's place. It'd been magical, and she truly believed he'd been as real as he was going to get. Some men hid things, like if they usually forgot to put the cap on the toothpaste, they'd do it when you slept over, but the second you were gone, they'd go back to being their old self.

She didn't think Luke was like that. Sure, he forgot things, like he was always losing his keys, even though his grandmother had a hook by the back door. But until she'd gotten her key bowl, she'd been the same way. She snapped her fingers, realizing the perfect present for Luke for Christmas.

She was just putting the last of her items away when there was a knock on the door. Smiling she walked to the door, hoping it was Luke.

She opened the door and saw her mother standing just outside on the landing in the dim light as the rain lightly fell. Then a tall, thin man stepped forward, and when the light hit his face, Amber knew her worst nightmare had come true. She looked into the eyes of the monster she'd feared for the last seventeen years.

Luke felt a little winded as he walked up Amber's stairs. By the time he made it to the landing, he was breathing hard and a light sheen of sweat was on his forehead. When he knocked, Amber answered quickly, looking ragged. Her eyes were red and she had a lost look on her face.

"Amber? Is everything—"

"Luke!" She grabbed his hand and pulled him in.

When he stepped in, he saw the couple. The woman looked small standing next to the tall, frail-looking man. The couple looked like an ad from the fifties, in their old-fashioned clothes.

"Luke, these are my parents, Donna and Frank Kennedy. This is Luke Crawford, my boyfriend." Amber grabbed his hand in a vice grip.

Luke nodded his head. He didn't know what was going on, but he guessed she'd been as shocked by her father's presence as he was.

"Amber, this isn't a conversation for guests. We don't mean to be rude, Luke, but it's a family matter."

He was about to say that he understood, but he wasn't going anywhere, when Amber broke in. "Anything you want to say, you can say in front of Luke. He's my family now." Her chin came up and he swore he'd never seen her look more beautiful than that moment.

Her mother's eyes went to Luke's and he saw them heat. Her father looked like he'd rather be anywhere but there.

"Fine." Her mother's lips thinned, and she crossed her hands in front of her. "As we were saying, we think it's time you came home. You've gotten out of hand. We understand you're a full-grown woman, but in Eugene you can be closer to your father and me. You need direction in your life; you haven't had any for so long. When I was here the last time, it was apparent to me that you've been living in sin. And living in this town, above a grocery store, no less. Now that your father is home, we can be a family again." She looked to her husband and smiled. For the first time, Luke could see the woman's eyes soften. "You can be there to help support him as he recovers from this mess. We can be there to help you clean up your life."

"Clean up my life? Be a family?" Luke felt Amber's hand vibrate in his. Gently he squeezed it, trying to give her some of his power, what little he had left. "Who do you think you are? I've got news for you, Mother." Amber dropped Luke's hand and walked over to face her mother, her face inches from the older woman's face. "You were never there for me, and I don't want you to be. You've done nothing over the last seventeen years to prove to me that you cared one bit for me. All you cared about was getting this devil from his cage." She waved her hand at her father. I thought I was raised by one monster, now I know I had two of them. I told you last time I wanted nothing to do with you. I mean it now more than before. If I ever see either of you again, it will be too soon." She walked over to her front door and held it open. "Leave."

Both her parents stood there looking at her, then looking at Luke. He nodded his head in agreement. He tried to look tough, but he was so angry, he may have come across looking more like a rabid dog. Both her parents walked out without saying another word.

Luke collapsed on to her couch as he heard her slam her door and flip the lock. Then she was by his side.

"Luke? You look terrible." She felt his forehead. "Oh my God! You're burning up." She rushed to the kitchen and came back with a cold wash cloth.

"I'll be okay. Amber?" He took her hand and looked into her blue eyes. They seemed to be floating in the darkness that was quickly overtaking him. "Amber? I want to be your family and for you to be mine."

"Luke, let me call Dr. Stevens. You're sick."

He shook his head and almost blacked out completely. "No, I want to be your family, and I want you to be mine."

"Luke? Luke?" He heard her voice fade as the darkness overcame him.

# Chapter Eighteen

Amber called Aaron with shaky hands. She'd pushed Luke back onto her couch as he'd passed out, thankful that he'd had enough sense to sit down. She'd seen the sick look, the pale skin, and hollowed out eyes when she'd opened her door, but her parents' presence had taken priority. Now, however, as she talked to Aaron, panic almost took over.

"I don't know," she tried to answer Aaron's questions. "He just showed up, pale, weak, and burning up. Then he passed out."

"I'll be right over." Aaron hung up.

Amber kept running the cool cloth over his forehead and face. Then she tried to take his jacket off, but it was hard to do with his dead weight. She almost spilled him onto the floor, so she gave up trying.

Then she heard the knock on the door as Aaron called for her.

Aaron rushed in after she unlocked the door and took one look at Luke. "Yeah, it's been going around." He shook his head. "I'll bet he's dehydrated, too." Aaron started taking Luke's vitals. "When was the last time you saw him?"

"Well, right before he went to play basketball with you. I thought he was going to come over last night, but..." She trailed off, feeling guilty that she hadn't called him to check up on him. She'd just assumed that he'd wanted some space.

"Don't worry. We'll get some fluids into him, and he'll start feeling better. I think the worst is over by now." Aaron opened a small pack and snapped it, then waved it below Luke's nose.

Luke came off the couch almost swinging. "Easy!" Aaron jumped back. "Lacey will kill me if I come home with another black eye from you," he joked, then looked at Amber and winked.

"What?" Luke sat down and grabbed his head in his hands. "Who hit me?"

Aaron chuckled. "The flu bug. It's been going around. Those kids we played the other day all ended up in my office the next day. Snot-nosed little brats gave it to everyone else." Aaron smiled.

"Yeah, well, next time we play healthy kids, not sick ones." Luke looked up at Amber. "Where your parents really here?"

She nodded. "You don't remember?"

"Sorta. In my version, they were missionaries trying to get you to convert to their weird religion."

"Close enough." She sat next to him. "I showed them the door. Hopefully, I'll never hear from them again." She reached up and felt his head. "Can you give him anything for the fever?" She asked Aaron.

"I took some aspirin." Luke leaned back on the couch.

"That's good." Aaron pulled a bottle out of his bag. "Did you have fluids with that aspirin?"

"OJ."

"Not so good. Water, good clean water is what you need. The OJ is okay for sugars and vitamins, but you're dehydrated."

"I slept for eighteen hours straight."

"That will do it. Amber, can you get him a glass of water?"

She rushed to the kitchen and came back with a large glass. "Here." She handed it to him and he downed half of it.

213

"Maybe you can stay with him, make sure the worst is over?" Aaron suggested.

"Yes, of course." Amber smiled.

"Good, well, if he gets worse or if his temperature stays over one hundred for too long, give me another call." Aaron looked at Luke and pointed at him. "You. Fluids, fluids, oh and—that's right— fluids." He smiled and walked out.

"You are such a fool." Amber leaned back. "If you ever scare me like that again..." She glared at him.

"Me? I almost had a heart attack when I walked in and saw the pilgrim couple trying to convert you. How did your father get out? I thought you said they needed you to spring him free?"

Luke finished the glass and set it down on her coaster. Then he leaned back on the couch and closed his eyes.

"Yeah, well, I'm not sure. I almost had a heart attack myself. Coming face to face with the devil will do that." She shivered and looked around the room. Somehow the place felt dirty now.

"I hate to ask it, but I think I'd feel better back at home."

"Say no more." She sprung up. "I was just looking for an excuse to get out of here. How about I take you back to your place and make you some of your grandmother's homemade chicken soup?"

214

He stood up and she reached to steady him. "I'd say, hell yes." He smiled.

When they arrived at his place, she took her overnight bag up to his room while he lay down on the couch with Jackie. She noticed the large Christmas tree in the front room and flipped on the lights for him to watch as he rested. It made the place feel more welcoming.

When she walked past the kitchen, she noticed a smaller tree in the back room. He'd hung a large wreath on the front door, and there was fresh evergreen garland wrapped around the banister. There were large red bows and lights as well. The place looked and smelled like Christmas.

When she walked into his room, though, the smell of sweat hit her. She decided a fresh change of sheets was called for.

From the look of his bed, he'd slept like a rock. Half the sheets were soaked in sweat and the other half of the bed was still made. She found a fresh pair of linens in the hall closet. When she was done, she carried his dirty linens down to the laundry room and started the load. She walked by the front room and saw he was fast asleep. She set a glass of water by him on a TV stand, then went into the kitchen and got to work on making him some soup. Half an hour later, Jackie paddled in and asked to go out. When she opened the back door, she realized it was snowing again. Standing on the back deck, she watched Jackie wander around the dark yard. Luke had installed a few motion lights, so the whole yard lit up, and she could easily see Jackie doing her business. The grass had just a light dusting of snow and the smell of winter hung in the air. She always enjoyed this time of year. The peace and quiet of the snow falling and the crisp feel of the cold wind on her face always made her feel more alive.

When Jackie was done, she wiped her paws with the towel Luke had hung by the back door. Jackie paddled back into the front room, no doubt to crawl back onto the couch with her master.

Amber continued to roll the homemade noodles and even watched some Christmas shows on the television as she worked. She'd never made noodles this way before, but the recipe sounded so good. She knew Luke needed the extra energy to help fight off the sickness. While she was boiling the chicken meat to release it from the bones, Iian text her.

*"Heard Luke is sick. Don't worry about coming in for the next few days. I'll cover for you. Take care of my best friend. --Iian."*

"Well, Luke, it's a good thing you have friends in high places." She smiled at the screen. Now she had the whole weekend off. She was actually looking forward to spending her time with Luke, even if he was sick.

When the soup was ready, she walked into the living room to wake him. He'd sweat through his shirt and the blanket she'd covered him with.

She forced him to drink a whole glass of water. He complained a little, but complied. When she brought him a large bowl of soup, he looked at it and shook his head.

"I'm not hungry." He tried to lean back.

"Luke, Dr. Stevens told me you needed chicken soup. I've spent the last hour in your kitchen rolling dough and making homemade chicken soup for the first time. You are going to eat every last bite, if you want to get any better."

His head hung, "Yes, ma'am. I'm sorry, Amber." He took the first bite she held in front of his nose. "Mmm, just like my gran used to make." He took the spoon from her and started scooping it into his mouth.

"I know, I used her recipe."

His head perked up. "There aren't any brownies in the oven right now, are there?" She actually saw his eyes sparkle for the first time since seeing him on her doorstep.

"No, but if you're good, I'm sure I can manage a batch. Maybe after you shower."

He looked down at his clothes. "Yeah, I guess I could use another shower."

When he'd finished the whole bowl of soup, she helped him upstairs and into the shower. He didn't even try to pull her in with him. She stood on the other side of the glass doors and watched as he showered.

"I don't want you falling and cracking your head open, so if you feel weak, just sit on the bench there." She pointed to the tile seat along the back wall of the shower.

"I'm fine. That soup helped a lot." When he was done showering, he pulled on a pair of old sweats and crawled back in bed.

She went back downstairs and got to work on making him brownies. After all, according to his grandmother, *"Chocolate cures all."*

When she came back upstairs, he was fast asleep. It was just past ten and her head and back hurt so she decided to crawl in next to him. In his sleep, he pulled her closer to his side. The dog jumped up on the foot of the bed. Amber took a deep breath and wished she could stay there forever, tucked in Luke's arms.

Luke woke to a bright light in his eyes. His head ached a little but for the most part, he could tell the flu had passed. He was extremely hot on one side and when he looked over, he saw Amber fast asleep next to him. Reaching up, he felt her forehead and closed his eyes.

Great! He'd gotten her sick. He pulled his arm out from under her head. "Amber?" He ran his hands over her heated skin. She moaned and tried to pull away, shivering. He grabbed the glass of water from the night stand. She must have left it there for him last night. Grabbing the bottle of aspirin from his night stand, he shook one out and tried to wake her again. "Amber? Honey, you need to drink this." He had to set the glass and the pill down to pull her into a sitting position. Then, when her eyes opened slightly, he forced her to down the pill and drink the whole glass. She immediately lay back down. "I'm sorry, honey."

"It's okay. I knew I'd get it. That's the price of being in love." He knew she was fevered, but hearing those words leave her mouth shook him. He must have stood there looking down at her for ten minutes.

Was she in love with him? He'd known how he felt about her for a while, but hadn't been sure what she felt. His mind raced as he walked into the bathroom and grabbed a cold washcloth for her forehead. Sitting beside her, he tried to cool her forehead and arms. She tried to push him away, her teeth chattering and goose bumps rising over the skin he was trying to cool.

"No, please." She pushed his hand away.

"Sorry, sweetie, I need to cool you down. You're burning up." Finally, when she settled back down and fell asleep again, he laid the cloth over her forehead and went downstairs to let Jackie out.

He saw a large container of soup in the fridge and heated up two bowls. Grabbing a bag of rolls, he carried the bowls up on a large tray. He'd brought a tall glass of orange juice, just in case she wanted some.

He forced her to down the entire bowl of soup and enjoyed every drop of his. Back downstairs, he heated up a second bowl for himself. He couldn't believe how perfect she'd made his grandmother's homemade soup. It had been years since his gran had made it. Closing his eyes, he could just see his gran standing in the kitchen, rolling the dough and cooking the meat off the chicken bones.

When he opened the fridge to put the rest of the soup away, he noticed a large container with a lid on it. He hadn't seen it before. He pulled it out and almost dropped it when he pulled the lid back. Brownies. He grabbed a knife and cut a huge piece off. When he bit into the rich goodness, his heart soared. He sat down and finished off his brownie, then he let Jackie out and watched her play in the yard. He went back up to check on Amber, and as he stood over her and watched her sleep, he knew he'd never let her go after this.

He let her sleep for a few hours, then checked on her again, making sure she drank plenty of fluids. He decided a shower would be just the thing for her.

He knew how unsteady he'd been on his feet, so he helped her to the bathroom, then stripped down and joined her, holding her up as the spray worked wonders on both of their sore muscles.

"Did you mean what you said?" She leaned her head against his chest.

"What?" He ran soapy hands over her hair.

"That I'm your family?"

He didn't know what she was talking about, but to him it sounded good. "Sure, sweetie." He tilted her so the spray cleaned the shampoo out of hair.

"Mmm, that feels good. I want you to be my family, because my family sucks." He looked down into her face and could see that her blue eyes were cloudy. He felt her naked body next to his, and the heat was almost unbearable. He turned the water temperature down a little, trying to cool her skin.

"No," she pulled closer to him, wrapping her arms around him. Her teeth started to chatter. "It's too cold."

"Sorry, baby, but I've got to bring your temperature down. You don't want me to call Aaron and have him give you a shot, now, do you?"

"No." She buried her head into his shoulder. "Take me to bed. I'm so tired."

"Okay, baby. Just a while longer." He kept her next to him until he felt her skin start to cool. Then he carried her into his room, and laying her on top

221

of the comforter, he quickly changed the sheets around her. Once half the bed was made, he moved her over to the clean side and covered her up as he fixed the other side. When he checked her again, her temperature had fallen, and she was fast asleep.

He sat down at this desk to get a few things done, and it was close to midnight before she stirred again. He'd woken her several times to push fluids into her, but this time, he heated up a bowl of soup.

"Wow, this is really good." She sat up in his bed, spooning the soup she'd made him into her mouth. "I think it tastes even better the day after you make it."

"Funny, I've always thought so, too. Gran used to freeze it in these small containers to keep some handy, and I always enjoyed it even more the second time around."

"Maybe that's why I ended up making so much. I followed her recipe and ended up with a huge pot full. Next time I can freeze some."

He smiled. "As long as you promise me some. I think it should be some sort of rule that I get some of everything you make from that box."

She looked at him, "Did you eat all those brownies?"

He laughed. "No, I was good. Do you want some?"

"Mmm, actually, a big slice of brownie does sound really good right about now."

"I bet we can find some old TV shows to watch, if you want? I'll get the brownies; you find the shows."

"Sounds like a date." She fluffed the pillow next to her.

They sat up in his bed, eating brownies and watching old Gilligan's Island reruns. He'd never had a better date with anyone.

# Chapter Nineteen

It took Amber a few days to recover from the flu. It had gone around town and half the staff of the Golden Oar had been out that week with it. Even Aaron had caught it and had to call in a doctor from Edgeview to cover his clinic until he recovered.

When she finally made it back to the Golden Oar, she was shocked to see the progress. The back room was painted, the ceiling tiles were in, and they were working on putting in the new hardwood flooring. They had promised to be done in the next day or so. All that would remain were the finally touches.

The fish tank was set to be delivered and set up on Monday. Everything was going to be ready for the Christmas party just a week away.

Since she'd taken last weekend to be with Luke and had been knocked out with the flu, she'd neglected her Christmas shopping, so she changed schedules with Thomas and cut out early one day to head into Edgeview to get caught up. She didn't have a lot of people to buy for, mainly Luke and Jackie, but she did want to get each of the Jordans something small and something for each of the staff members she'd become close to.

She enjoyed the short drive to Edgeview, and by the time she was returning home, snow was steadily falling. The Christmas party was now just a few days away, and she felt she had plenty of time to wrap all her presents. When she got back, she spent an hour precisely wrapping each one and placing them under her tree. Even with the lights going and Christmas music playing, there was still something missing. Amber sat in the dark watching the lights and listening to the Carpenters sing about roasted chestnuts, and missing Luke and Jackie.

The next few days flew by fast. Luke had called her and confirmed that he'd be taking her to the party. He'd apologized that he hadn't been able to be around more, telling her he had a small side project that had been keeping him busy. She tried not to imagine him locked in a game, an endless battle on his computer screen, like Chris had always been.

The back room of the Golden Oar was finished and ready for the grand opening. Iian had locked the door and only allowed Lacey and Amber in to decorate for the Christmas party. The men were installing the fish tank that day, but since she was helping Lacey, she couldn't oversee their work.

"So, what's the deal with you and Luke?" Lacey asked while hanging decorations.

Amber almost coughed. "Well…"

"Don't mind me. I may not like being gossiped about in town, but that doesn't mean I don't like knowing what's going on with a close friend." She turned back to her decorations.

"I know Luke means a lot to your family. I honestly don't have any intentions of hurting him." She stood there, not knowing what to say to Lacey.

Lacey stopped what she was doing and looked at her, her brow furrowed and a slight frown on her face. "I was talking about you, friend. At least I'd hoped we were friends. The last few days, working with you, I could tell you've been preoccupied with something. I just figured it had to do with Luke. I don't need to go over there and kick his butt again, do I?"

Amber's eyebrows shot up. "Yes…no…I mean…I love that you're my friend, I'm honored. No, you don't have to kick Luke's butt." She looked at the small five-foot-tall woman standing there with her hands on her hips. "You didn't really kick his butt, did you?"

"No, but I did gave him a fat lip once. Of course, we were playing basketball." They both laughed.

"I don't know what's going on with Luke. I've had such wonderful times with him, two wonderful weekends I've spent at his house." She sighed.

"What's the problem, then?" Lacey went back to her decorations.

"Well, my fear that he's a man-boy in hiding."

"A... man-boy." Lacey laughed so hard she grabbed her sides. "Man-boy. Luke?"

"Well, yes." Amber watched Lacey try to stop laughing.

"Amber, Luke is the most responsible person I know. Sure, he and my brother like to goof off every now and then, but when he moved back to Pride, all boy-like qualities were taken away. Honestly, I think he's more mature than my husband and both my brothers rolled into one."

"But...the video games? My last boyfriend was addicted like Luke is, and I'm just not ready to continue competing with a man who stays up all night to fight aliens."

Lacey looked at Amber like she'd grown a second head. "Do you know what Luke does for a living?"

"Yes, he told me."

"He told you what, exactly?" Lacey put down the large bow she'd been holding.

227

"Well, that he worked for the company that made the computer games."

Lacey walked over to her and took her hand, then pulled her to the back game room area that Iian had overseen. The small room housed several stand-up video game consoles. One of them had a very familiar-looking alien on the front. Alien Engagement was written in bright purple letters across the front. The yellow planet Odge was in the background as Modark stood defending the side of the unit.

"Honey, this is Luke's baby." Lacey pointed to the new machine.

"What do you mean?" She stood there looking at the impressive looking game.

"It's his. All his. From starting project to finish. He's Modark. Creator, inventor, programmer, defender. When he moved back to Pride, he needed something he could do to support his family without leaving Pride. So he and a buddy from MIT decided to create Modark. Less than a year later, they went public with it and well, the rest is history. His buddy runs the business side of everything while Luke creates, programs, and comes up with the games. Honey, Luke is no man-boy. He's simply a man-genius." Lacey walked away leaving Amber to look at the shiny new machine and the spitting image of Luke as an alien that stared back into her eyes. The alien's copper eyes were a dead giveaway. She didn't know why she hadn't see the likeness before. She'd been a fool, and she owed Luke an apology.

The night of the big Christmas party came, and Luke was excited and nervous. Tonight he'd put himself out there.

"It's all or nothing." He looked down at Jackie as he fixed his bow tie. "If I don't do it tonight, I'll know I'm chicken and won't be able to live with myself." Jackie whined and sat on her bottom, her tail wagging. "Sorry, girl. You've got to stay home tonight. But if all goes well, Amber will be coming back home with me." When he said Amber's name, Jackie stood up and pranced to the door, looking around. "No, baby. She's not here, yet."

When he drove up to Amber's apartment, his palms were sweaty and he felt his heart skip a few beats. Then she opened the door and his heart stopped.

She wore red—tight, glorious red. Her dress had a low V neckline that showed enough cleavage to make his mouth water. The thin straps that held the number up begged to be pulled down, and her soft skin begged to be touched and kissed. Her heels were tall enough that she and he almost looked eye to eye. Her dark hair was pushed up on top of her head with wisps falling around her face. She wore silver dangling earrings that caught the light when she turned her head.

He must have stood outside her door for a full minute before he could finally breathe.

"Well, I'll take that as a compliment." She laughed.

He nodded his head. His tongue still felt tied up, and he was afraid if he tried to talk, it would fall out like in the cartoons, when the wolf's eyes would bulge out and his tongue would roll out and lay on the floor.

"Well, do you want to come in or should we head out?" She held up a dark coat and looked at him questioningly.

"In...um...if I come in, we may never go to the party," he finally said, sounding like a fool as he stuttered.

"Then you can help me on with my coat, and we can go." She handed him her coat and turned around, showing him the back of her dress. The material plummeted to the middle of her back and he stood there with her coat in his hands, staring at her soft skin, desire hitting him full force.

She looked over her shoulder and smiled. "Luke?" His eyes traveled back up to her face. Her lips were as red as her dress and he couldn't stop himself from watching her tongue dart out and lick them. "Are you going to help me on with my coat or not?"

He nodded his head and held out his hands as she slipped the coat on. When her skin was covered, he blinked a few times and tried to steady his breathing. She turned around and smiled, and he knew he was a goner. There was no way he was going to make it through the night. "Can you carry the presents?" She nodded to a large bag full of wrapped boxes. He had a bag of presents to hand out himself in his truck.

When they reached the restaurant, he pulled close to the door and let her get out with the two bags of gifts. "I'll park the car and be right back." She nodded and rushed under the awning. He found a spot near the back of the lot and rushed through the snow to where she stood waiting for him. Shaking the snow from his hair, he smiled and held out his hands for the bags. "Shall we?"

"Yes, I'm so excited." They entered the restaurant, and he was amazed at the transformation. Gone was the family friendly restaurant, and in its place was a winter wonderland. He helped Amber off with her coat and then removed his. Soft Christmas lights hung from the ceiling, making everything glow.

He spotted Iian and Allison right away. They stood a few feet from the door, greeting everyone. There were several employees standing around taking everyone's coats and taking all of the presents to a large Christmas tree that sat by the fireplace near the back. Other employees were handing out drinks to guests.

After talking to several friends, Amber pulled Luke towards the bar to show him the fish tank. He could tell she was excited that it had turned out so well. The blue lights and exotic fish looked good.

Then she pulled him into the back room where most of the guests were gathered. A large Christmas tree stood in the center under a large disco ball. There was a band playing on the stage, and people were slowly dancing around the tree to Christmas music. He saw several of his friends dancing with their wives and some dancing with their children, spinning around the room playfully.

He could see kids of every age. Most of the little boys were in the back room playing video games, while the little girls danced around in pretty dresses with either themselves or a parent.

"It's wonderful. Just what the place needed. And to think," he said, pulling her close and swaying gently with her, "that none of this would have happened without you."

She smiled up at him. "I owe you an apology." Her smile slid away a little.

"Oh?" he leaned in to kiss her red lips softly. "Why?" He looked into her blue eyes and watched the bright lights reflect in them.

"I didn't know what you did. That Alien Engagement was yours." She frowned as he chuckled.

"So you found out I don't play video games for a living, huh?" He kissed her lips again. "It doesn't matter."

"Oh, but it does. I treated you like a man-boy and made fun of what you did for a living. For that, I'm sorry."

He smiled down at her. "It doesn't matter," he repeated. "What matters is that you're here with me. That even after thinking I was a man-boy," he chuckled, "that you still took a chance to be with me. To be part of my family, as you called it." He pulled her closer. "I wanted to give you a gift, later. But now seems like the perfect time." He took a deep breath and pulled a small box from his pocket. Her face dropped and her hands dropped to her sides.

"Amber?" He knelt down right there in the middle of the new dance floor with the whole town of Pride looking on. "Will you do me the honor of moving in with me?" He opened the box and there was a silver key on a piece of tinsel in the box.

She laughed as he stood up, and then she hugged him. "Yes! Yes, I'll move in with you."

He laughed and spun her around. When he set her back down she looked at the box. Then she frowned. "Actually, now that I think about it. No." He sobered and his heart stopped. The music had stopped and now they had everyone in the restaurant's attention. "No, I won't move in with you." She looked up into his eyes. "Not until you say that you'll marry me."

He heard a few of his friends laugh. "She beat him to it," someone said from the crowd.

233

He smiled, and this time when he got down on his knee, he presented a smaller box. "I was hoping to ask that question next." He opened the lid to a beautiful silver ring with a simple cut diamond in the middle. It was an old-fashioned ring, and the sparkle of all the lights almost blinded her. "It was my grandmother's." He pulled the ring out of the box and slid it smoothly onto her finger. "Amber Kennedy, will you move in with me? Be my family? The mother to Jackie? And to some human babies maybe a few years down the road? Will you marry me?"

She smiled and nodded, then pulled him up and kissed him until the cheering around them slowed and then stopped.

*If you've enjoyed this book, please consider leaving a review where you purchased it. Thanks! --Jill*

*Want a FREE copy of my Pride Series novella, Serving Pride?* **Join my newsletter** *at* jillsanders.com *and get your copy today. You'll also be the first to hear about new releases, freebies, giveaways, and more.*

**Follow Jill online at:**

Web: www.jillsanders.com
Twitter: @jilllmsanders
Facebook: JillSandersBooks
Email: jill@jillsanders.com

# Epilogue

Amber stood in the backyard watching Jackie play as the snow fell. She heard the back door open and close and felt Luke's arms come around her. She leaned back into his warmth and smiled.

"Did we get everything?" he asked her.

"Yeah, that was the last of it. I can't believe it's all here."

He chuckled. "It pays to know a basketball team of kids to help you move. Even if they did break your key bowl. Sorry about that," he mumbled.

"That's okay. The one I bought you is big enough to hold both our keys." She smiled.

"It was fate that you bought one big enough." He kissed her hair.

"No, not really. I knew I would end up here, one way or another." She turned into his arms. "Did you get everything moved into your new office, okay?" She snuggled into his chest.

"Yeah, our bedroom is now Modark- and Korkin-free." He chuckled. "Plain old boring bedroom."

"Well," she said looking up at him, "we'll just have to make our own fun in there from now on."

His eyes went to her lips, and he pulled her towards the door. "How about we get started on that right now?" She laughed as they rushed into the house and up the stairs together.

# My Sweet Valentine Preview

# Prologue

Allen struggled to hold the Blackhawk steady. He could hear the bullets flying by and, for just a second, he closed his eyes and prayed. Then he took a deep breath and pointed the nose of the chopper where he needed to be. Signaling his crew, they were in position, he held his hands steady as his men extracted the marines from the site.

All his concentration was on keeping the bird steady. His crew was working on the last marine when he felt the sting in his chest. The bird jolted to the side as debris from the tempered glass flew around his face, hitting his helmet and knocking off his face shield. Warning sirens went off, signaling that the chopper was in trouble. His crew screamed in his ear as he gripped the stick with both hands, which was slick with his own blood. His vision threatened to fade, so he bit the inside of his cheek and held on. Looking behind him, he saw that the last marine was safe, so he pointed the bird into open skies.

"Allen!" his co-pilot Mayer yelled at him in the headset. "You got this?"

"Yeah. I got this." The sound of gunfire faded away as they hit open sky. His chest was on fire and breathing was getting difficult. He felt the chopper tilt and heard a new group of alarms going off. This time he knew there was no way to pull the bird up from the nosedive.

Yelling to the back for everyone to hold on, he relayed his location information to base as they spiraled out of control towards the desert floor.

A second before impact, his mind flashed to a peaceful image of him sitting on a beach somewhere, a large, hairy black dog running in the surf after a stick, a woman's gentle hand touching his arm. The second he turned to look at her, the bird hit the desert floor. Pain exploded in his body until all he knew was darkness.

When he surfaced again, it was to his crew screaming his name. Private Steven's was standing over him, yelling for him to get out. Then the next minute, the man was dead, hunched over the console, half his face gone from a round. The shock tried to force Allen to freeze up, but he'd been trained for this. Since his body was sheltered from the incoming rounds, he stayed down. Looking behind him, he could see the other men in his team looking at him for instructions.

"Stay down. Stay put until we see where it's coming from," he said into his headset.

"The ridge on the left. We've tried to get the shooter, but he's in there tight." Lt. Miller, their sharpshooter, sounded pissed. "He picked off two of the marines before we could get behind cover."

"Damn." His team had risked their lives for those marines and to have two of them gone while he was out just pissed him off. "Is there only the one shooter?"

"Yeah, we landed in a pretty remote area. Base says Humvees are en route."

"Miller, do whatever it takes to take him out. I'll cause a distraction. When he pops his head up, take him out."

Allen reached around and unbuckled himself. Slowly he slid to the left and out of the seat. He could see the desert floor jutting up into his view. In the distance, he saw a flash a second before Miller's shot rang out. The hidden sniper's bullet grazed his helmet as Miller's round took him down.

"Better stay down, just in case there's more." Allen looked around the desert hills and after a few minutes of silence, everyone relaxed and waited for the convoy to come pick them up.

Allen sat there quietly waiting for rescue, bleeding through a hole in his side, dreaming of a beach, a dog, and a woman.

# Chapter One

## Five years later...

Allen was caged in again. Every time he turned to get away, there was another opponent. They were faster, smaller, and younger than he was. Even though they were well matched in numbers, his crew was about to get their butts whipped. He went in for a kill, only to get stuffed and served.

"Get behind him, let's try that one again," Aaron, his captain, said as they huddled together. "We've got these twerps. We aren't going to let a bunch of greasy-faced teenagers take us down, are we?"

"It's now or never." Allen knew they had to gain the higher ground again. He looked around, trying to avoid the watchful eyes, knowing the distraction could end up killing them.

"Break." They parted ways as the buzzer sounded the timeout was over.

When the ball was in motion again, he realized there was no way they were going to win. Those greasy kids were going to whip their butts. They made three more points to the teenagers' five before there was a squeal, causing the entire gym to look towards the bleachers.

"Aaron, your wife's water just broke. You better get over here and take her in. You're having a baby," said Megan Jordan. She stood by the petite Lacey Stevens, who was past her due date and stood there holding her protruding belly. Aaron, along with Lacey's two brothers, Iian and Todd, rushed off the court and lifted her down gently from the bleachers. Luke and Allen stood there trying to catch their breath. They smiled and watched their friends all hover as Aaron carried his wife out the doors. Several of the women who'd been cheering them on left.

Two women remained. They talked as the other team and the referee left.

"Is that Amber, the new manager for the Golden Oar?" Allen slapped Luke's back as he looked at the pretty brunette. He kept trying not to look at the raven-haired beauty standing next to Luke's new girl.

"Yeah." Luke smiled in her direction. Allen knew Luke and Amber had been seeing each other for about a month. Luke's grandmother had died recently and he'd been going through a rough time. But seeing Luke's smile and watching his eyes light up when he looked at Amber, he knew he'd gotten through the hardest part.

The black-haired beauty standing next to Amber had been introduced to Allen before the game as Sara Lander, an old friend of Allison Jordan's. Sara had been born and raised in Pride, but for the past three years had been living in Seattle. He didn't know much more, but curiosity was killing him.

Luke waved to Amber and started to walk towards the locker rooms. Allen followed him, trying to keep his eyes from traveling to the two women standing by the bleachers. He couldn't understand why he was feeling a pull towards Sara, but he was, and he was the last person to deny an instinct.

"So, you grew up here?" Allen asked while the two men showered in separate stalls.

"Yeah, I moved east after school and spent some time at MIT." There was a moment of silence. "Why?"

"Well, I figured you could fill me in on what you know about Sara." He tried to sound casual, but his friend easily caught on and for the entire time they were in the showers and getting dressed, Luke gave him shit over it. He did get some useful information from his friend, but Luke spent most of the time getting back at Allen for all the shit he'd given Luke over the last few weeks about his feelings towards Amber.

With the tables turned, Allen knew he was in for it. He just smiled and returned the humor when he could.

When they walked out to the gym, Allen was a little disappointed to see Amber standing there alone, waiting for Luke. He watched the couple leave and felt a twinge in his chest. Why did it feel like he'd found everything he'd been dreaming of that fateful day when his chopper had gone down except the one thing he desired most?

He walked out, then hopped in his truck and checked his messages while his truck warmed up in the parking lot. He enjoyed his job as company commander of the new Coastguard base. When he'd arrived that first day to check out the facility, he'd walked out on the beach and sat on a large piece of driftwood. He'd known instantly that he'd found the right spot. It had taken him several months to tie up loose ends and find a place to live. He'd been lucky to find an older house just on the outskirts of town that needed a little work. It had been easy enough fixing the house up. The new headquarters for the Pride Coastguard was a different story; it had taken almost a year to turn the old sawmill into the top-notch facility it now was.

Over a thousand recruits had come in and out of the front doors of that place last year. So many that they'd turned one of the outbuildings into barracks to house all the recruits. Now, less than a year later, they were building another, larger building to the south of the original facility to house even more recruits. They were also adding a large kitchen facility along with a medical center. The small town of Pride was growing bigger thanks to the Coastguard, and Allen was in charge of it all.

There were those in town who didn't want over two hundred recruits running around town, but for the most part, people seem to appreciate the change and the added notoriety that came with having the Coastguard at their doorstep.

Even though the facility only housed the school, they had an active branch that could, at a moment's notice, whisk away to be out on a call. Allen had gone on a dozen or so calls in the last year alone. Most of them were fishing boats that needed help. Some were recreational vehicles that had gotten themselves in trouble. But, to date, Allen had not felt the stress and pressure that he had overseas.

Allen drove off through town and noticed someone standing out in the rain on Main Street. When he looked closer, he realized it was Sara. He quickly pulled over, his first thought being that her car had broken down. But when he pulled up, she turned from looking into an empty building and waved at him.

Sara stood on the sidewalk in front of the large building, looking into the windows. The empty building was dark, but if she cupped her hands, she could see all the way to the back of the empty room. It was huge. Bigger than she needed. Her heart skipped a few beats as she mentally designed the space.

She heard a car drive up and turned and watched Luke get out of his truck and open the door for Amber. Sara had just met Amber a half-hour ago at the gym while they watched the men playing basketball. Apparently, she was the new manager at the Golden Oar.

Sara had been visiting Allison to see her and Iian's son, Conner. Allison was one of her closest school friends. When she'd gotten there, Allison had invited her to go watch the guys play a game against some teenagers at the Boys and Girls Club.

"Hi." Sara waved to them and walked across the street. Luke looked at her like she was crazy for standing out in the cold, and she explained, "I was just driving by and saw the 'for sale' sign and thought I'd stop and look."

"Are you in the market for an old building?" Luke asked.

She laughed. "Yes actually, I've been thinking about opening a bakery." Sara turned back towards the building. "It's a lot bigger than I'd planned, but I think it'll work." She turned back towards them. "I could even have tables in the front and offer breakfast items. The Golden Oar is great, but they don't open until lunch. I could sell coffee, donuts, and muffins. Not to mention cakes and pies."

Luke took Sara's hand in his. "Marry me." He laughed and she could see the humor in her old friend's eyes. He'd always been a joker.

"Luke, you know I'd never marry you." She laughed and punched him on the arm. "Do you know if Allison's family still owns the building?" She'd never thought to ask Allison before. She knew her friend was probably busy at the hospital with Lacey and their family.

"I think so, but you might want to ask next time you see her. I expect a party the second that baby arrives. Maybe this time tomorrow?" Luke took Amber's hand and Sara realized she was probably holding them up.

"Yeah." Sara bit her lip and turned back towards the building. "Maybe I will ask her." She turned back towards them and said, "I didn't mean to interrupt your plans. Have a great night." She turned and walked back across the street.

She felt a little sad as she watched her friend walk up the stairs on the side of the local mart. She knew there was a large apartment Patty O'Neil rented out. When the lights turned on in the apartment, she turned and walked back to the empty store and realized she could now see into the empty building even better.

Leaning her face against the cold glass, she didn't hear the second car approach until it passed her and stopped on the wrong side of the street right next to her.

"Did your car break down?" His voice was deep and instantly she felt warmth spread up her spine. Turning, she looked up. It was dark inside his truck, but she could make out his profile. She'd seen him for the first time half an hour ago and she still felt the shock from that first view. Taking a deep breath, she walked over to his truck and placed her friendliest smile on her face.

"No, just looking at an empty building. Thanks for stopping though." She hoped he'd drive away soon. Being this close to him was doing something to her. She was actually shaking.

"Can't you look at it in the daylight when it's not this cold out?" His voice was laced with concern.

She smiled again. "I guess I'm used to the cold." She tucked her hands into her heavy coat pockets. Her gloves were keeping them warm enough, but she was beginning to feel the chill. "I can't really see anything tonight anyway. Thanks for stopping and checking on me."

She could see him frown. "Why are you looking at an old building?" He looked behind her at the empty spot.

If she kept telling people, no doubt the news of her business venture would be all over Pride before she got a chance to talk to Allison about the space. "It used to belong to Allison. I'm just checking up on it."

He frowned again and looked down at her. There was an awkward moment of silence. "Well, I'll wait until you get in your car."

She huffed out her breath. He really wasn't going to leave until she got in her car. She felt like he was babysitting her. She was an adult. She could take care of herself. Pulling her shoulders back, she turned and walked to her car and got in. His truck lights blinded her as he sat behind her car. It was after six in the evening in Pride, and everyone was having dinner, tucked nice and warm in their homes.

She pulled her keys from her coat and turned them only to have her car sputter as she tried to start it. She'd just gotten a tune up before she'd left Seattle. She punched the gas pedal a few times with her foot and tried again. She could feel the lights from Allen's trucks boring into her back.

"Come on! Start. Don't embarrass me in front of him." She tried again, only to have her car completely stop making any noise. "No, no, no. Don't do this. Please." When she tried again, she realized it wasn't going to happen.

She jumped when he knocked on her window. He stood outside, his coat and hat sheltering him from the light snow that had just started. She leaned over and rolled down her window.

"Won't start?" He leaned closer.

"No." She looked down at her car gauge. The engine light was on.

"Might need a new battery. If you want, I can take you home and you can deal with it in the morning."

She looked straight ahead and felt the shaking starting again. "No, that's okay. I live just a few—"

"Lady, I wouldn't let my worst enemy walk a block in this weather. Gather your stuff up, I'll drive you wherever you need to go." He opened her door and stood back, waiting for her to get her things.

Again, she felt like she was left no choice. She knew he was the commander at the Coastguard, so he was probably used to getting his way. That didn't mean he could boss her around. She gathered up her purse and decided everything else in the car could wait until the morning.

When she got out, she realized how tall he was. She had to look up to him when she spoke. "It's very nice of you to offer, but I'll be just fine. I only live two blocks away."

"I'm just trying to be neighborly. I'm Allen Masters, by the way. We weren't formally introduced." He stood there and smiled at her. She felt a little of her resolve melt; he had a great smile.

"Yes, I know. I'm Sara Lander. It's nice to meet you."

During the basketball game, Allison had told her all about Allen. How he'd come into town and taken charge of all the construction, turning the old mill into the newly renovated facility the Coastguard now used. Apparently, he was also a pilot and went out on rescues all the time. Surely she could trust someone who risked his life every day to save others.

"Well." She looked up at him and realized how good looking he was. Too much man, she thought. She felt like a teenager standing next to Tom Selleck in his heyday. What would she do with a man like him? She'd only dated one person seriously before and he didn't look like this. Allen was probably in his early thirties. His dark hair was covered with a ball cap with a Coastguard patch. His brown leather coat looked loved and worn in places. His jeans were the same, faded and worn out.

According to Allison, he'd been overseas in the war. She probably had nothing in common with him. He most likely found her to be irritating. Especially since she'd kept him standing on the sidewalk for a few minutes now.

Pulling her bag close to her, she nodded her head and raised her chin. "Fine. You can drive me home." She started walking towards his truck and thought she heard him laugh. "Did you say something?" She turned and looked at him, her eyebrows raised in question.

He smiled. "No, ma'am." He rushed to the passenger side of his truck and opened the door for her. She stood there looking at the large truck, trying to figure out how to get in it.

"If you grab onto that handhold there, you can step on the running board and pull yourself in." He smiled.

She did as he suggested. It took her two tries to pull herself into the large vehicle. As he walked around the front of the truck, the heat hit her full force and she realized she was freezing. Her teeth started chattering the second he opened his door. She clenched her jaw to keep from letting him know how cold she was.

"I'm sorry, I guess I didn't realize how tall my truck is." He smiled at her and she could tell he was trying to hold back laughter.

She nodded her head, not wanting to open her jaw in case her teeth should start banging together. He pulled into Main Street and started driving up the hill slowly. "Where to?" He looked over at her.

"Two blocks up, one to the right." The warmth inside the cab was quickly heating her. When he looked at her, she felt heat spreading from her insides as well.

"So, are you going to tell me why you were really looking at the empty building?"

She quickly looked at him, trying to figure out how he knew she'd lied to him. When he just continued to smile, she told him.

"I'm thinking of opening a bakery. Well, I've been thinking of it ever since I saw the empty building." She looked out the window. He was driving too slowly for her liking.

"Bakery, huh?" She turned and saw him looking straight ahead, thinking. "Are you any good at baking?"

"It does help to be good at it, in order to run my own bakery." She laughed.

"I like that." He smiled at her and she felt her stomach flutter.

"What?" She tried not to notice how nice his smile was. "That I can bake?"

"No, your laugh." He glanced at her again. "You should do that often."

She frowned a little. She didn't know what she should do now. Thank him? She was saved when he continued on.

"What kind of things would you sell in your bakery? Cakes? Brownies?"

"Yes, a little of everything. The nearest bakery is in Edgeview. They do a lot of cake orders for birthdays, weddings, and everything. But I was also thinking of doing sandwiches. Cold and hot."

"Do you know how to make bagels?" He shook his head. "I haven't had a good bagel since Boston."

She laughed. "Yes, actually, they are one of my favorites as well."

He looked over at her and smiled. "I'd do just about anything for a loaded bagel with whipped strawberry cream cheese on top."

She imagined exactly what she'd like him to do, causing her cheeks to heat. "There, it's the last house on the left." She turned her face away, hoping he hadn't noticed them turn bright red.

He pulled into the drive and quickly got out. Before she could gather her bag, he was opening her door and holding his hand out for her to take.

She put her gloved hand in his while trying to step down on the running board, but ended up falling forward straight into his arms. His muscled arms wrapped around her and she felt how solid his chest was against her own. He smelled of shampoo and leather, a wonderful combination. She looked up and started to apologize, her face so close to his she could feel his breath on her face.

"I'm—" Then his lips were on hers and she forgot where she was and what was happening. He tasted like heaven and just the feel of his warm mouth on hers sent every remaining chill from her entire body. Not only did she forget to breath, she forgot to move and stood encased in his arms like a statue as his mouth moved over hers.

He pulled back and smiled down at her. "Sorry, I must have slipped."

She would have laughed if she'd regained any of her senses, but instead she just nodded her head and lowered her eyes to the V of his jacket.

What did someone do with someone like him? A more sophisticated woman would have laughed and flirted with him. But she was having a hard enough time putting two words together to make a sentence.

Just then the front porch light went on and she pulled out of his arms, almost slipping on the ice in her driveway.

"My mother." She didn't know why she'd felt the need to explain things to him, but he smiled and dropped his arms.

"Well, if you can't get the car started in the morning, give Rusty a call. He'll fix it up for you real fast." He shoved his hands into his pockets.

She hoisted her bag over her shoulder. Everyone from Pride knew about Rusty, the only mechanic in a thirty-mile radius. Sara didn't know what to say, so she just nodded and started walking towards the front porch, then stopped and turned around.

"Thanks for the ride." She didn't want to seem rude. Her mind had just clicked into gear and she realized she was about to walk away without thanking him.

He nodded and smiled. "Anytime." He turned and got back into his truck, waiting in the driveway until she was safely inside.

When she closed the door, Becca, her sixteen-year-old sister jumped on her. "Who was that?" She sat on the edge of the couch and peered out the front blinds.

"Allen Masters. My car wouldn't start, and he stopped and offered me a ride." She tossed her bag onto the couch and walked into the kitchen to find her mother sitting at her desk in the corner, working on her computer. Her mother looked more like Becca than Sara. They had the same build, tall and skinny. Her mother's short gray hair looked stylish and her silver earrings bobbed up and down. Her mother was a chain smoker, but had recently quit. Now she chose to compensate by chewing on Nicotine gum all the time. "Evening, Mom. What would you like for dinner?"

It had been the same every night for the last several weeks since she'd gotten home. If Sara didn't cook dinner, Becca and their mother would eat something microwaved that had more chemicals in it than the boxes the food was packaged in.

Even though she loved her family, she was ready to find a place of her own. Becca had been allowed to run wild since Sara had left several years ago. It wasn't Becca's fault, really. Their mother had spoiled her from the moment she'd been born. Sara, on the other hand, had taken over the parent role since the fifth grade, when their father had packed his bags and moved to Vegas with their mother's best friend. Neither Becca nor Sara had seen him since.

"Whatever you want, dear. I can always heat something up."

"No." Becca jumped in, walking over to the countertop. "Sara doesn't mind cooking, do you?" Her sister was a lot taller than Sara's own five-foot-five frame. Not to mention she had more curves than her and her hair was lighter than her own. Basically, Becca was the pretty child. Sara had curly, raven hair, but she'd never really looked at it as beautiful, just a nuisance to take care off. Mostly, she kept it tied back out of the way as she baked. Tying it back now, she got to work making spaghetti for her family as she thought of Allen Masters and the kiss that had baked her insides.

**Other books by Jill Sanders**

**The Pride Series**

**The Secret Series**

**The West Series**

**The Grayton Series**

Last Resort
Someday Beach
Rip Current
In Too Deep
Swept Away

**Lucky Series**
Unlucky In Love
Sweet Resolve

For a complete list of books:  http://jillsanders.com

RED HOT CHRISTMAS

DIGITAL ISBN: 978-1-942896-25-8

PRINT ISBN: 978-1-942896-26-5

Copyright © 2013 Jill Sanders

Copyeditor: Erica Ellis – inkdeepediting.com

# About the Author

Jill Sanders is the New York Times and USA Today bestselling author of the Pride Series, the Secret Series, and the West Series romance novels. Having sold over 150,000 books within six months of her first release, she continues to lure new readers with her sweet and sexy stories. Her books are available in every English-speaking country, available in audio books, and are now being translated into six different languages.

Born as an identical twin in a large family, she was raised in the Pacific Northwest. She later relocated to Colorado for college and a successful IT career before discovering her talent as a writer. She now makes her home in charming rural Florida where she enjoys the beach, swimming, hiking, wine tasting, and, of course, writing.

Made in the USA
Coppell, TX
15 April 2021